THE MYSTERY OF
THE RUSSIAN RANSOM

RICHMOND HILL
PUBLIC LIBRARY

MAR 2

RICHMO
905-7

BOOK SOLD
NO LONGER R.H.P.L.
PROPERTY

ROY MACGREGOR

Tundra Books

Text copyright © 2014 by Roy MacGregor

Published in Canada by Tundra Books, a division of Random House of Canada Limited,
One Toronto Street, Suite 300, Toronto, Ontario M5C 2V6

Published in the United States by Tundra Books of Northern New York,
P.O. Box 1030, Plattsburgh, New York 12901

Library of Congress Control Number: 2013940759

All rights reserved. The use of any part of this publication reproduced, transmitted in
any form or by any means, electronic, mechanical, photocopying, recording, or
otherwise, or stored in a retrieval system, without the prior written consent of the
publisher – or, in case of photocopying or other reprographic copying, a licence from
the Canadian Copyright Licensing Agency – is an infringement of the copyright law.

Library and Archives Canada Cataloguing in Publication

MacGregor, Roy, 1948-, author
        The mystery of the Russian ransom / by Roy MacGregor.

(Screech Owls)
Issued in print and electronic formats.
ISBN 978-1-77049-420-6 (pbk.). – ISBN 978-1-77049-425-1 (epub)

        I. Title. II. Series: MacGregor, Roy, 1948- . Screech Owls series.

PS8575.G84M99 2014   jC813'.54   C2013-903542-7
                                                C2013-903543-5

Designed by Jennifer Lum

www.tundrabooks.com

Printed and bound in the United States of America

1 2 3 4 5 6   19 18 17 16 15 14

For Craig "Flash" Gordon,
the King of Monday Night Hockey.
Teammate, friend, lover of family,
and the Detroit Red Wings.
May he skate forever.

1

My name is Sarah Cuthbertson. I am twelve years old. I have no idea where I am or what is going to happen to me. I am frightened.

I do not know how long I can write this without being caught. I do not know if I can even get this message out to anyone. In fact, I know nothing at all about what is going on or what this is all about. I am really, really scared.

We were on our way back to the hotel from the rink in Ufa. My hockey team, the Screech Owls, had just finished their very first practice in Russia. We didn't have the greatest workout – Muck said we were all suffering from jet lag and we should get back to our rooms and get some rest. I'm sharing with Jenny Staples, our backup goaltender, and Samantha Bennett – Sam – who is one of my two best friends on the team.

But I wasn't tired. Nor was Travis, who is my other best friend as well as the captain of the Owls. It was a beautiful day outside. There wasn't a cloud in the sky, and the sun was so bright it was sparkling on the fresh snow. Travis said we should walk back to the hotel while the others took the bus. He asked me if I would show him how to do this silly move I've been practicing. I just discovered it in practice last week when we went onto the ice right after a fresh flood. The pucks were still kind of wet, so I put the back of my stick blade on the puck, pushing down hard, and then quickly twirled the blade up so that it lifted the puck off the ice and left it sitting on top of the blade. Then I flipped the puck in the air and batted it straight into the net! A total fluke, but some of the Owls saw it and went crazy, banging their sticks on the ice.

Apart from that, Travis, as team captain (I'm assistant), wanted to talk about how we could make sure Nish (the other assistant captain) didn't get one of his insane ideas, like mooning the crowd or replacing the Russian flag at the rink with his stupid boxer shorts, and get the whole team in trouble. We are in a country where we don't even speak the language (except for Dmitri Yakushev, of course, who lived in Russia before his family moved, and who plays right wing on the same line as me and Travis), and so we better assume that people might not appreciate a nut bar like Nish.

It wasn't a long walk, just through Yakutova Park across ulitsa Lenina – which Dmitri says means "Lenin Street" – turn left on ulitsa Karla Marksa and keep on going for several blocks until you reach the Hotel Astoria, where the team is staying.

Muck said he had no problem with us walking. So Travis and I went off across the street at the light and headed in through the high arch that leads into the park.

We were just starting to talk about how to keep Nish under control when we got to this eternal flame that burns in the center of the park. There was a high stone monument there with names carved into it, but because Travis and I couldn't even figure out the alphabet, let alone the language, we had no idea what it meant.

I was taking a picture of Trav standing next to it when he suddenly shouted for me to run.

I turned just in time to see three large men coming fast toward us. All three were wearing dark tracksuits and had black balaclavas covering their entire heads except for the eyes. I could see the eyes staring straight at us.

I thought there must be some mistake and they were going to run right past us, but before I could even take a step, they were on top of us.

One of the men knocked Travis down and pushed him hard into a snowbank that had been shoveled next to the monument.

The other two grabbed me. One of them pulled a dark cloth bag over my head.

After that, I could see nothing but darkness.

I screamed, but it sounded muffled, like I'd fallen into a well or something.

I heard Travis screaming for help, but that was muffled, too, and then I heard nothing.

I knew they were carrying me fast – I was bouncing on someone's shoulder and it hurt. I struggled, but he was way too strong for me and it only made him squeeze tighter.

They threw me into a car or a van. I could feel leather seats and they were warm – the vehicle must have been waiting for them, its engine already running.

A door slammed hard behind me. Then another door and another, and then all I could hear was the tires spinning in the snow as the vehicle pulled away.

I have no idea where it took me. And no idea what will happen to me.

I'm scared.

2

*W*ake up! *Wake up! WAKE UP!*

Travis Lindsay was running through the park, and as he ran he tried to force himself awake. His boots were slipping on the ice, the fresh-fallen snow spilling in over the tops and sliding, cold and wet, down around his ankles.

If I can feel that, he told himself, this must be real.

But it couldn't be real! It had to be a nightmare! It made no more sense than those dreams he would have as a little kid where green witches were chasing him and his feet sank into mud so he couldn't run.

But he was running now. He could feel his feet slipping, his heart pounding, and his chest burning. He could hear his own breath, rasping and crying at the same time. He knew there were tears in his eyes. When he blinked, he could feel them freezing along his temples and down each cheek.

What else could it be but a nightmare? He had seen three men running toward him and Sarah. He had felt one of them crash into him with the hardest check he had ever felt off the ice. He had lain there moaning as he tried to catch his breath, and seen the two other men grab Sarah, pull a dark cloth bag over her head, and race off with her back behind the bushes where they had been hiding.

When he got to his feet to go and help her, the man who had hit him struck him again. This time Travis spun and crashed face-first into the snowbank. Everything went black, then cold, as the snow slithered down his neck.

By the time Travis pulled free and shook the snow out of his eyes, the men were gone. He could hear car doors slamming and the whine of tires trying to get a grip on the snow and ice.

And then there was nothing. No Sarah. No men wearing tracksuits and balaclavas. Nothing.

It *had* to be a nightmare.

But there was no waking up from this dream. He had never been so wide awake in his life. Travis knew this was real and that something horrible had just happened.

He ran through the park toward Karl Marx Street. He had to get to the hotel. He had to tell Muck what had happened.

Travis was running and crying, his feet trying to move so fast that twice he slipped and went down on the icy path. He ran past the little amusement park – closed up for the winter – and through the gates, slipping again as his boots sought traction.

A man saw Travis fall and hurried over to help, but Travis was already on his feet and yelling. *"I need help! Someone has kidnapped my friend! Can you please help me?"*

The man just stared at Travis, baffled. He said

something, but Travis had no idea what the man was saying.

Travis had no way of explaining. Hand signals might work for food and directions, but what hand signal could possibly say three men wearing balaclavas had just taken a twelve-year-old girl in broad daylight and made off with her?

Travis knocked snow off his leg and started running again. The man who had stopped to help stared after him as if the youngster were some sort of madman.

Down the streets, Travis ran, slipping and sliding, sometimes falling. He was forced to slow down where the sidewalks had yet to be shoveled and the snow was high. Whenever he saw a break in the cars, he moved out onto the road and ran along the side of the plowed street.

He could see the hotel. His chest was burning with pain. His eyes were stinging. *How was he going to explain? What were they going to do?*

3

I am trying to figure out what is going on here. I am in a sort of cell. It's not a jail cell. I have a bed and a dresser. It is hardly a dungeon – the bedclothes are fresh and even pretty: red flowers on a pale yellow background. There is a picture on the wall, a nice winter scene with kids skating on an outdoor pond. The room is actually quite comfortable, almost like a hotel room, with a washroom and a shower off to the side. But there are no windows.

And the door is locked.

So far, I have seen only a woman. Or at least that's the only face I have seen. The men who took me here in the car kept their faces hidden. I have no idea what they look like. But the woman hid nothing. She had on sort of a nurse uniform. She never smiled when she set me up in this room. Never smiled once. But she wasn't mean or anything, just never smiled.

She went through my backpack. I think she was looking for a cell phone, but I don't have one. She left my diary. She left the book I am reading. She left the deck of cards we used on the flight over to play Fish. She left my mirror and toothbrush and toothpaste and the little scissors I carry for my nails. I guess they aren't worried about me trying to fight my way out of here!

Someone is coming.

It was the woman again. She was pushing a cart, and now I have a meal in front of me. I'm not as terrified as I was when the men grabbed me, and I'm not as scared as I was when they put me in this room. That doesn't mean I'm not worried – I still get frightened when I think about it. But I don't think they plan to poison me – or starve me. In fact, the food smells good, though I really don't feel like eating.

The soup is called borscht, she said. It is red and has cabbage in it and it's delicious. The other plate is meatballs and spaghetti, and it's delicious, too. They gave me pop to drink – a sweet orange pop. I'd rather have juice.

But that's a silly complaint when I think about it. Would I rather be dead in a snowbank in the middle of nowhere or drinking pop that's too sweet? I'll take the pop, thanks.

I think there is a one-way window in the door. There's frosted glass there, and I can't see out. But I think they can see in – otherwise, why have the window? But if someone is watching me, they know I'm writing in my diary, and no one has tried to stop me.

What is it they want with me?

Someone is coming again.

That was weird! It was the woman again, but this time she smiled. I thought the smile looked fake, like she was trying to pretend everything was all right, when obviously it isn't. I didn't smile back.

She speaks very good English. She has a strong accent, but I can understand her fine. "I have something for you, Sarah," she said when she came in.

She knew my name! How could that possibly be? She didn't take my wallet from my pack when she went through it. And my name isn't anywhere on the pack.

But she knows my name. She used it twice.

"Sarah, we want you to change into these," she said.

She was carrying a bag. She opened it up and pulled out a bunch of athletic stuff. Underclothes and a tracksuit. She laid it all out on the bed, smiled, and left the room. I heard the lock click behind her as she left.

I sat for the longest time. I didn't know what to do. But then – curious, I guess – I held the clothes up to me to see if they would fit. It looked like they would.

I went into the washroom so I'd have a little privacy and put the clothes on. They were all brand-new and smelled fresh. And everything fit perfectly!

I looked in the mirror and actually liked what I saw. The tracksuit is bright red but has a small emblem over the heart. It's golden and looks like a two-headed eagle or something. I know I have seen it somewhere before.

But why a tracksuit? Do they expect me to work out in this little room?

Someone is coming again.

4

"Okay, Travis," Muck said very carefully. "Slow it down, young man – and let's start again at the very beginning."

Travis closed his eyes and took several deep, long breaths. He brushed his light brown hair back from his forehead. It was soaking wet from his run. He felt his heart slowing down. It was still racing but no longer pounded in his chest.

The *beginning*, yes. But even before the incident in the park, there was the trip to Russia. Even before Sarah was kidnapped, it was already the most incredible, bizarre trip the Screech Owls had ever undertaken.

It began with Dmitri Yakushev's uncle. Dmitri's family came from Leningrad, Russia – which used to be called Saint Petersburg, and now is called Saint Petersburg again. Travis and the rest of the Owls soon learned that nothing is simple in Russia.

Coach Muck Munro, who is a history nut, told the Screech Owls' parents that some guy named Winston Churchill once said, "Russia is a riddle wrapped in a mystery inside an enigma." That made Travis's mom and dad nod with approval, and there were murmurs of agreement all around the room where the Owls' parents had gathered to talk about maybe going to Russia.

Travis looked back at Nish, who was sitting just behind with his mom. Nish's face was beet red and so twisted that it looked like someone with huge hands had just tried to wring his neck. Nish could never sit still. Travis thought they shouldn't even try making him.

Travis knew exactly what his best friend was thinking: What the heck does *that* mean? Travis knew what a riddle was. And he knew, of course, what a mystery was. His grandmother was a great fan of Agatha Christie, who must have written more than a hundred mysteries, and Travis loved the Sherlock Holmes mysteries on television. But an *enigma*?

Maybe Muck was talking about this man who had approached the Owls about coming to Russia. The man knew Dmitri's uncle. The Yakushev family had a connection right back to the famous 1972 Summit Series, when Paul Henderson had scored the most famous goal in hockey history. The best player and top scorer on the Soviet Union team had been Alexander Yakushev, a relative.

Dmitri's father had talked to the parents about how different the Russia of today was from the Soviet Union of 1972. Back then, Russia was seen as the enemy. There was only one political party, the Communist Party, and whoever was head of the party was a dictator. The people had no power and no say. They were very poor, because most of the country's money went into military operations and spying on countries like the United States and Great Britain. The Soviets and Americans were so often on the verge of fighting each other that it was called the Cold War.

"In Russia today, people have the vote, just like here," Dmitri's father told the parents. "And communism has been replaced by American-style capitalism to the point where there are bigger malls than anything we have here. Everyone wears fur," he said, maybe exaggerating a little, "and, just like us, everyone drives a Japanese car."

Anyway, Dmitri's uncle had contacted Dmitri's father with an idea. The Screech Owls would be invited to Russia by the City of Ufa and this man called Ivan Petrov. Ufa was a city of more than a million people, but none of the Owls' parents knew anything about it except that it was the site of the 2013 World Junior Hockey Championship, which the United States had won over Sweden. Canada and

Russia had played for the bronze medal and Russia had won that game, leaving Canada in fourth place.

Ufa, however, was where a lot of oil came from. Dmitri's father said it was a bit like Calgary or Dallas – a place with enormous wealth.

And this was where Mr. Petrov came into the picture. He was a billionaire – "That's like being a millionaire a thousand times over," explained Data – and was so rich that even if he did nothing but hand his money out, he couldn't spend all of it. He had made his money in oil, but his big passion was hockey.

Mr. Petrov, Dmitri's father explained, had become Russian hockey's greatest benefactor. He had helped out members of the old 1972 team, who were getting elderly now and many of whom were sick. He had also given a lot of money to hockey development, particularly to the Russian junior hockey program and to women's hockey in Russia, which, unlike men's hockey, lagged far behind other countries in international competition.

Mr. Petrov had heard about the Screech Owls and the fact that some of their best players were girls – Sarah at center, Sam on defense, Jenny in goal – and wanted to bring them over to Russia so that the people who ran hockey there could see the benefits of having girls and boys play together at young ages. He believed that this was what had made Canadian and American women so dominant in women's hockey – with either the Canadians or the Americans taking the gold medal in each Winter Olympics.

His offer was simple. He would pay for flights and accommodation for the entire Screech Owls team. No need for the usual big bottle drive or selling chocolate bars door-to-door to fund this trip.

Muck Munro was harder to convince than the kids. Once the Owls heard about the possibility of going, they couldn't contain their excitement. Nish even announced he might set his all-time record for mooning people in Russia. Sam said she hoped he would so they'd throw him in jail and toss away the key and she'd never have to look at his ugly butt again.

The parents met and held a vote. They were all for it, even if not all of them would be going along. Parents had to pay for themselves, and it was expensive. The team would stay together at the Astoria; parents would have to find their own accommodation elsewhere.

Muck began to come around after Dmitri's father stressed the historic significance of where they were going. Ufa might be unknown in North America, but it was famous in Russia. In the months following the Russian Revolution of 1917, it had been a place of great power. And it had been founded nearly five hundred years ago, Dmitri's father added, "by Ivan the Terrible."

Travis saw Muck's eyes light up at the mention of this name. He knew at that moment that the Owls would be taking up Mr. Petrov's generous offer.

Travis swallowed hard.

Ivan the *Terrible*?

Wasn't he, Travis Lindsay, distantly related to Hockey Hall-of-Famer "Terrible" Ted Lindsay?

Maybe Travis was *meant* to go to Ufa.

5

"And that's the last you saw of her?" Muck asked. Travis nodded. His lower lip was trembling; his eyes were stinging. He couldn't stop the tears. He felt no shame. He felt only that he had failed Sarah.

Muck and Mr. Dillinger were blurs and swirls of color as Travis stared at them through his tears. He wiped his eyes hard with the backs of his hands. Mr. D stepped forward, his thick mustache twitching, and took Travis's head in his hands and hugged him against his ample stomach. Travis burst into sobs.

"You did everything you could, Travis," Mr. D said. "They were three grown men. You can't beat up on yourself."

Travis had described what happened as best he could: the walk, the stop for photos at the monument, the men running, their balaclavas and tracksuits, the first blow that knocked him over and the second blow that almost knocked him out.

"You couldn't make out any of the faces?" Muck asked. Muck was so calm, his voice so comforting, even though Travis knew the coach had to be as worried as everyone else.

Travis shook his head.

"Mr. Yakushev has gone for the police," Mr. D said. "I've called the parents at their hotel, and they're on their way over."

Mr. D was doing what Mr. D did best: organizing the details, being a friendly presence. He was the perfect team manager.

Muck was doing what he did best: staying calm, quietly talking things over, not panicking. Travis had no idea how Muck did it. He never seemed to change. The coach had sat only two rows ahead of Nish and Travis on the jet that flew them across the Atlantic Ocean to Heathrow Airport in London, then three rows ahead of them for the Aeroflot flight to Moscow, then just across the aisle for the long flight to Ufa. They had traveled for more than thirty hours, but Travis never once saw Muck asleep. He sat there, reading a fat book on the czars of Russia, while others slept and watched their little televisions. A few times, Travis saw Muck get up and stretch his legs, especially the one that he'd injured in junior hockey, but the rest of the time, he just sat up straight and read his book.

Something about Muck's calm manner settled Travis down. He was no longer sobbing.

There were sounds in the hallway. People. Both Russian and English being spoken. He could hear Mr. Yakushev's voice speaking both languages.

There was a knock at the door and Mr. and Mrs. Cuthbertson burst in. Mrs. Cuthbertson was crying, which caused Travis's eyes to start watering all over again. She ran to Travis and squeezed him so hard Travis thought he was going to burst.

Right behind the Cuthbertsons came Mr. Yakushev, Mr. Petrov, and two uniformed police, one a man and one a woman. They looked very serious.

Mr. Petrov, the billionaire who had brought the Owls to Russia, looked worried sick. Travis knew he would be blaming himself. But so would Muck, who had let Travis and Sarah walk back to the hotel alone. But the real person to blame, Travis knew, was himself. He'd suggested they walk back through the park. He'd failed to protect Sarah from the men.

"I am so happy you're safe," Mrs. Cuthbertson said as she kissed Travis's cheek. "I know you tried to help our Sarah."

Travis broke inside. What good was *trying* when you were a twelve-year-old boy? And a small twelve-year-old at that? He had failed his friend, his line mate.

Mr. Cuthbertson put a big hand on Travis's shoulder and gently pulled his wife away. He smiled at Travis and mouthed the words *thank you*. Travis could see that Mr. Cuthbertson was trying hard to be calm and not look scared. But Travis could see the fear.

"The police do not believe any harm will come to Sarah," Dmitri's father told Muck and Mr. D. "They are convinced this is a ransom kidnapping. Unfortunately, with all the new wealth in Russia now, it sometimes happens."

Muck and Mr. D nodded, seemingly comforted to hear that it was about money rather than causing harm to Sarah. Money was only money. Sarah was much more precious.

"Travis," Mr. Yakushev said.

Travis looked in his direction, his eyesight still blurred from the tears.

"Travis," Mr. Yakushev continued, "do you think you could tell us again what happened? Right from the beginning? I will translate for Mr. Petrov and the police. Go slowly, and try to remember absolutely everything that happened, okay?"

Travis nodded. He knew his voice would sound small and childlike. He could feel it in his throat even before it came out. But he also knew he had to, for Sarah.

He began to tell his story all over again.

6

I am back in the room. There was a meal waiting
for me. Sort of pierogies – cheese and bacon
inside them. They were good. And this time an
energy drink. Not so sweet. Perfect.

I have time to write in my diary again. I can
tell what happened, so far, but I don't have a clue
what any of it means. It is weird. I don't know if I
should be scared or not. The only thing I know for
sure is, I WANT OUT OF HERE! When I think of my
dad and mom and how upset they must be, I start

to cry. When I think about Muck and Mr. D and how worried *they* must be, I start to cry. When I think about Travis and if he's hurt from that man hitting him, I start to cry. When I think about anything, I start to cry. So better not to think and just write down what happened.

I had the red tracksuit on with the golden double-headed eagle crest. I had new Nike track shoes, top-of-the-line.

The woman came to get me. She says I can call her Olga, but she didn't give a last name. She keeps smiling at me, but I refuse to smile back. I don't trust her.

We went out into a long hallway and down some very twisting corridors. I didn't see a single person the whole time. Just Olga and me.

We came to a door and she opened it. We walked through a long corridor. It was cold. It was sort of like being in an arena. We followed some turns in the corridor and came to another door, which Olga opened and indicated I should go in first.

It was warm inside and the room was very large and open. There was an office area where some people were busy on computers. I was tempted to call out to them, but something made me hold back. They never even looked up as Olga hustled me past them. It was as if I wasn't even there. We came to another door, and she opened it up and motioned to me to step through.

It was a full gymnasium. There were treadmills and weight machines and gymnastic mats and stationary bicycles and every workout machine you could imagine.

But no one was working out.

A man and a woman came walking across the gymnasium floor. They had white coats on, almost like doctors. They acted friendly and they knew my name, though they did not tell me their names and they seemed to know very little English.

I was weighed and measured by them. Not measured just for height – they took so many measurements of me. They measured my waist, thighs, calves, butt, chest, arms, hands, feet. I thought for a moment they were going to build an actual life model of me out of clay or something.

Then they had me run on the treadmill. But

first they hooked up a tube and a mask so that everything I breathed in and out was being measured.

They ran me until they could see my heart rate was at a certain level and then they slowed the machine so that it stayed at that high rate for several minutes. When they told me to stop, I almost fell over. I was so sweaty, and my legs felt like jelly.

But they wanted more. I lifted weights for them. I did flexibility tests for them. They even had me run in quick bursts around the gym, having me explode as fast as I could for a moment, then slow down as fast as I could. On my jelly legs, it was tough.

I noticed they were filming all of this. There were cameras all along the little track, and they worked by remote control. I could see them turning with me as I went by. I felt like I was being watched by a herd of strange-looking one-eyed creatures.

It gave me the willies.

7

"Get your equipment and be in the lobby in ten minutes."

There was something about Muck's orders that brought everything back down to earth. Travis's head had been spinning with all the horrors that might have befallen Sarah. Sam had been in tears virtually from the moment news went around the hotel that Sarah was missing. Even Nish had seemed out of sorts. He hadn't done anything stupid for hours – a slow day for Wayne Nishikawa.

Muck's words changed all that in an instant. Travis had a purpose. He was to get his equipment. They were off to the rink. He could hardly collect his bag and sticks fast enough.

By the time Travis reached the lobby with his equipment, the place was buzzing with activity. Mr. D was assembling the equipment bags in a pile for the shuttle bus and collecting the sticks together so they could be stashed underneath with everything else. Mr. Yakushev and Mr. Petrov were deep in discussion with the hotel manager, and the policewoman was with them. Mr. and Mrs. Cuthbertson were sitting at a coffee table, waiting. They seemed fairly calm.

Once Travis had dropped his equipment and sat down to wait for the bus with Andy Higgins and Lars Johanssen and some of the other players, Muck moved to the center of the lobby and blew his whistle.

"He thinks this is a practice," Nish hissed under his breath, giggling.

"Listen up, now!" Muck said, the entire lobby going quiet as he spoke. "We all know about

33

Sarah. Thanks to the police and Mr. Petrov, we have people out all over the city looking for her. No one knows what happened, but the police are convinced no harm will come to her. They believe they will be hearing shortly from her captors and that it will be a ransom case. They are looking for money. For Sarah's safety, the police have not contacted the media. They want to keep things quiet so that the kidnappers don't panic and do something stupid.

"As you may be aware, Mr. Petrov is a successful businessman, and the kidnappers must have known that he would consider the Screech Owls to be under his care while visiting his country. He is likely as much a target of this crime as Sarah is herself, and has already informed the police that he will pay whatever it takes to get Sarah back to us. This is for you to know but not for you to say. It stays with all of us in this room, understand?"

All around, there were murmurs of agreement and gratitude for Mr. Petrov's incredible gesture.

"Good," Muck continued. "If word got back that Mr. Petrov was willing to pay up, the ransom would just go up and up and up. So we say nothing and we wait.

"In the meantime, we are here for a tournament. Mr. D and the parents have all agreed that the best way for the Screech Owls to spend their time is not to mope around the hotel. We can't do anything at all to help the situation, and we know that our Sarah would want the Screech Owls doing what the Owls do best – playing hockey."

"*Yes!*" Data shouted. He did a small wheelie in his wheelchair by shifting his upper body and pumped a fist in the air.

"*Yes!*" some others shouted.

"*For Sarah!*" Sam shouted, her eyes still red.

"*Sarah!*"

"SARAH!"

Travis's world was right again – so long as he kept his mind from going in a certain direction that involved Sarah.

He was half-dressed, every piece of equipment put on in the proper order, a ritual he followed every time he dressed to play. He tugged his jersey over his head, pausing just as the *C* for *Captain* passed his lips to offer a gentle kiss from the inside that no one could see. He pulled on his helmet and tightened the chin strap. He pulled on his gloves, punched them twice and was ready.

Routine meant everything. He twirled his stick blade as he went out onto the ice. He was first through the far corner, digging in hard so his skates made a sound almost as if he were frying bacon in a pan in the morning.

Mr. D tossed the pucks over the boards. Still warm, they bounced and stuck on the wet ice. Travis tried that amazing little trick he had seen Sarah do back home in Tamarack. He almost managed to scoop the puck clean off the ice, but it slipped off the blade when he spun it and bounced away on him. He'd have to get Sarah to show him how. Once she got back. Once they got her back.

Travis shook his head hard, almost as if he could shake bad thoughts out of his head and they'd be gone forever. He picked up another puck but didn't try the trick. Instead, he skated in and pinged a shot hard off the crossbar.

He felt right once more.

Apart from the quick warm-up, there was no time for practice. They would start tournament play immediately. Sarah's disappearance had so upset the Owls that their first skate in Ufa had been canceled.

They had no sense of the rink, no feeling for the larger ice surface, no feeling of comfort. All of which was fine with Travis Lindsay, Screech Owls captain. This was a game. And the Owls were a hockey team. Playing hockey games was what they did. And every single one of them was glad for the distraction.

If Muck and Mr. D were worried, they didn't show it. Muck had somehow determined just from the warm-up that the team they'd be facing – a peewee team from Minsk – had a weak defense. Muck's instructions were, as always, simple and to the point: "Be strong on the forecheck. See if you can panic their defense into some turnovers."

Travis's line started, as it usually did. But without Sarah. Instead, Andy Higgins moved up to play center on the first line: big Andy with the long reach and the hard shot. He'd never skate as beautifully as Sarah did. He didn't see the ice as well as she did. But Andy was still an excellent player. Just not Sarah.

Dmitri, on the other side, was deep in concentration, staring at center ice as if his eyes were lasers trying to melt the circle. Nish, of course, was back on defense. Travis looked back just before the puck dropped. Nish was looking up into the crowd, almost as if he expected fans to be carrying signs for him.

The puck dropped, and Andy used his body to keep the Minsk center from getting to it. Dmitri swept it to the side and fired it hard into the Minsk end, the puck trapped at the back of the net by the little Minsk goaltender.

Travis was first in, remembering Muck's instructions. He went straight at the defenseman, who was looping back to pick up the puck. Normally, Travis would do what Muck called a fly past, cutting just in front of the goal to make sure the defenseman stayed back there and tried to pass rather than carry. But Travis came straight for him, not concerned in the slightest that the defenseman could use the net as an opportunity to cut Travis off and slip away on the other side of it.

The defenseman panicked, just as Muck knew he would. He tried to bounce the puck off the boards and keep it while Travis roared past, but Travis anticipated the move and dragged his left skate so that it picked up the puck. He kicked the puck forward onto his stick and fired a hard backhand cross-ice to Nish, storming in from the blue line.

Nish wasn't thinking about the crowd now. Nish was thinking about *Nish*. As in glory-hog, all-star, superhero, Hall-of-Famer Nish. He raised his stick high and delivered a screaming slap shot.

Travis, cutting back, saw that Nish's shot was going to miss. But then, seemingly out of nowhere, a stick blade flashed, ticking the puck ever so slightly, and it blew high into the back of the Minsk net.

Dmitri! He had ducked in around the defense-man to defend on the shot and somehow managed to tip the shot. Sometimes Dmitri's eye-hand coordination blew Travis away. He was so skilled, so fast.

Screech Owls 1, Minsk 0.

Travis and his line skated back to the face-off, but Muck sent out a new lineup and replaced Nish on defense with Fahd Noorizadeh.

Travis sat. He could feel Mr. D's big hand pinch the back of his neck. He could feel Muck lightly pat his shoulder. But Travis knew what it meant: good listening, good job.

Travis could also feel a huge emptiness beside him. Sarah should be sitting there. They should be tapping gloves after a nice play.

But Sarah was not there.

8

I did not sleep well. I cried myself to sleep think-ing of my mom and dad and how worried they must be. If only I could get a message to them! And I had a nightmare, a bad one.

The Owls were playing hockey. It must have been a tournament, because I didn't recognize the rink. The ice surface was huge; it seemed to go on forever – more like a frozen lake than any rink I've ever seen.

We were playing against a team that was really, really dirty. They were bigger and older than us, and they were going after all our little guys – especially Simon Milliken and Travis. At one point, they charged Travis so hard he went right through the boards. I don't know where the boards came from, because there were none when the game started. They had to bring an ambulance on the ice to take Travis away on a stretcher.

Every bone in his body was broken. His legs and arms were bent in all the wrong directions. His skates looked like they were on backward. The medics had bottles of blood dripping into his arms.

But then I saw Nish. He'd decided to streak the game and had come out in nothing but his boxer shorts and skates and Jeremy Weathers's goalie mask, and the other team was chasing after him and slapping his butt hard with their sticks. He was screaming as he skated past me – his chubby legs were churning like helicopter blades as he tried to escape.

I woke up crying and laughing. And then I realized where I was and I just kept crying.

I fell back asleep eventually. I don't remember

what I dreamed, if I dreamed anything, but I must have been asleep because I didn't notice that someone had unlocked the door and come in.

I don't know if it was Olga or not. All I know is that someone came in and put something on the floor at the end of my bed.

A hockey bag.

And inside, all brand-new equipment – exactly my size.

9

It had been the Dmitri Show. The Owls were still laughing about it after their 6–1 march over the team from Minsk. Dmitri had four goals – his hard backhand sending the water bottle spinning three times off the back of the net – and set Travis up for a five-point game.

Nish had scored the sixth and final goal on an end-to-end rush when he split the Minsk defense, pulled out their poor goaltender, and slipped the puck perfectly into the back of the net. Then, when

Travis, Dmitri, and Andy had skated toward him to tap his pads, Nish had burst right by them and skated hard to the blue line, where he went down on his knees and spun all the way up the ice.

Nish never saw the ice again. He sat like an angry troll at the end of the bench, his helmet off, his wet black hair smeared across his forehead, his face as red as a tomato.

Muck never said a word to Nish. That was Muck's way. He let his actions speak for him. He'd let Nish figure out for himself why he'd been benched.

When the horn sounded, the celebration was subdued. Travis felt bad for the outplayed Minsk team. He felt empty while tapping gloves with his teammates to mark the victory when Sarah wasn't there. The Owls lined up to shake hands with the Minsk players but without much emotion at all. For someone just walking into the Ufa Arena at this moment, it would have been difficult to say which team had won and which had lost.

With a stern warning that they were to stick together in groups of at least four, Muck let the Owls wander about the rink and the nearby shopping mall. He and Mr. D, as well as Mr. Yakushev and Mr. Petrov, were going to talk with the parents who had come to Ufa with the Screech Owls. Nish's mom hadn't been able to afford to come. Travis's parents had stayed behind, too, because Mr. Lindsay had a long-planned business trip to New York City and his mother had already bought tickets to two Broadway plays that she had wanted to see for years.

For the Owls' parents, the trip to Russia was expensive – Mr. Petrov's generosity only went as far as the team – and many of them had decided not to come. So, for the most part, the Owls were left to themselves.

Travis headed for the mall with Sam, Jenny, and Jesse Highboy. He knew that Sam and Jenny were having a rough time with Sarah's disappearance, and he thought they'd find some distraction over there.

The mall was brand-new. They went up the

escalator to the second floor and stared in disbelief at a little shop called Sniper that was selling handguns, pellet guns, crossbows, and even an assault rifle.

They went up another floor and found the food court, where there were takeouts offering all sorts of Russian and Ukrainian and Chinese food, but also a Subway and a McDonald's. All four of them wanted to try a Russian Big Mac and ordered the Big Mac meal. They might never have left North America: it tasted *exactly* the same.

In the basement level, the mall had a sort of farmers' market. The stalls held more meat and vegetables and fruit and candy than any of the Owls had ever seen in a store in Tamarack. They stood at the butcher's for a while and watched a burly man with a handlebar mustache wield a heavy cleaver as if it were an ax. He was splitting logs. He swung as high as he could and brought the cleaver down with a heavy thud on the side of what Travis thought was a huge pig. The butcher's white apron was streaked dark red with blood.

"*I will never eat meat again!*" Sam said loudly.

"I feel sick," said Jenny.

"You guys are silly," said Jesse. "Where do you think your Big Macs came from – out of thin air? I see this all the time when I go home to James Bay. But usually it's my grandmother swinging the ax. My grandfather's too busy gutting the moose or caribou or whatever it is he's killed."

"*I'm gonna hurl!*" Sam shouted, in a perfect impersonation of Nish.

The four friends stood there, laughing. It struck Travis that this was probably the first time he had seen Sam and Jenny happy since Sarah had disappeared.

And when they stopped, the emptiness returned.

Normally, Sarah would have been there to join in making fun of Nish.

10

I didn't know what to do with the hockey equipment. I checked it out – the very best Nike, Easton, and CCM stuff you can buy – but I didn't try it on. I couldn't figure out what it was there for. A gift? Something to take my mind off what was happening to me?

Olga came and told me I should get dressed in the equipment but leave my skates off. She left the room, so I went ahead and tried it all on. It was the nicest equipment I've ever seen.

I put my hair in a ponytail, pulled on the helmet, and checked it all out in the little wall mirror. It looked smart! Really, really nice equipment.

Someone's coming.

She returned to get me. I carried a skate in each hand and walked behind her, still wearing my new sneakers. We walked along a different hallway, and I could feel cold drafts from time to time, especially when we came to closed doors and opened them.

We entered another door that led to an arena. I couldn't see the ice, but I didn't need to. Anyone who has played hockey all her life instantly knows the smell of an arena. It is as distinctive as the smell of vinegar or banana – or Nish's disgusting hockey bag.

She took me into a room where a man was sharpening skates – again, a sound and a smell that are so completely distinctive to the rink. There was a wall of new sticks – Nikes and Eastons – all the top-of-the-line composite models.

The man didn't seem to know any English, but he made it clear with hand signals and smiles that I was to take my pick. I sorted through a bunch of lefts, took a curve I liked – the handle was stamped "N. Yakupov" – and the man held up two rolls of tape, white in one hand, black in the other. I picked black because Muck always said a goalie has more trouble picking up a black puck being shot by a black stick blade than a black puck coming off a white background. Makes sense to me, so I'm a black-tape player. I also tape my sticks toe-to-heel, like Muck does, while some of the Owls – Nish, for example, and Fahd – go heel-to-toe.

Once the stick was ready, Olga told me to put on my skates, which the man had carefully sharpened while I was taping my stick. He was no Mr. D, but he seemed to know what he was doing.

In a couple of minutes, I was ready. I was dressed exactly the way I most like to be dressed. I was wearing all the best hockey equipment I could imagine. I had a brand-new composite stick that weighed so little it could have been made of air. And yet I felt strange.

"Come, Sarah," said Olga.

I followed her out of the equipment room, turned left, and we walked to the ice surface. It was a beautiful new rink, international size, with good lighting and no windows. The only sound was the Zamboni leaving the ice surface and then the loud, hollow click of the doors closing to the Zamboni chute.

"Go ahead," Olga said. "Skate."

I went out in total silence. How different from heading out with your teammates. No crowd, not even a few parents, to cheer you. No opposing team to measure. No whacks on the shin pads and butt from your teammates. No team yell before the puck drops.

The fresh ice glistened. I skated around with my head down, just watching my new Easton skates make lovely parallel lines in the ice. I dug hard in the corners to see if I still had my usual jump. I did. It felt good to be back doing what I love most of all.

I checked out the arena, the penalty box, the benches. There were cameras, too, set every so often down both sides of the rink and in the corners. I couldn't tell if they were on.

What do they want of me?

The equipment man came down the corridor

with a bucket of pucks and tipped them out onto the ice.

I figured I might as well try out the new stick, so I went over and tried my new trick, banging the back of the curved blade down hard on the puck and, once it "stuck" a bit, flicking the puck up so I was carrying it. I did this a few times and then worked on flipping the puck into the air and catching it. That worked a few times, but it's something I'll need to work on if I hope to skate around the entire rink flipping and catching pucks like pancakes in a frying pan.

I heard noises and looked up. Two men wearing tracksuits and helmets came out onto the ice. They had skates and sticks and looked like coaches.

One spoke to me, and he knew my name.

"Hi, Sarah," he said. "My name is Pavel, and this is Sacha. We're going to put you through some drills, okay?"

What was I supposed to say? "*No way – and you can call the police right this minute!*"

It was better than sitting in my room moping. So we started passing pucks around and skating hard. They had me do some sprints up and down the ice – "bag" skates, Muck called them, and said he hated them when he was in junior – and then some agility moves carrying a puck through a series of pylons.

It was sort of like a skills competition – but one in which I was the only player.

Then I noticed someone watching at the far end of the ice. It was a tall man with a fur hat pulled way down, almost over his eyes. I could not see his face.

It gave me the shivers to look at him and know he was staring at me.

11

"You have *got* to be kidding me!"

Travis stared hard at Lars, but Lars was nodding his head wildly up and down, his eyes wide as bright blue pucks.

"*Seriously?*" Travis asked.

"Seriously," Lars confirmed.

The four Owls had come back to the rink and were waiting around for the shuttle bus to take them back to the hotel. Ever since the incident with

Sarah, Muck and Mr. D had banned them from walking through the park.

They had bumped into Nish in the hall near the souvenir stands and food kiosks. After Nish said he was going to find something to eat and wandered off, Travis, Sam, Jenny, and Jesse went into the stands to watch the game going on – a peewee team from Finland up against one that came from Kazakhstan. Dmitri was there, watching the play intently.

The team from "Kaz," as Dmitri called it, was actually pretty slick and well coached. Dmitri said they played the old "Soviet" system of hockey – units of five, defense and forwards rotating as the situation demanded – but Travis wasn't sure what he was talking about. Like Muck, Travis wasn't much for using fancy words and phrases to describe how a game was played. It never seemed to need words when you were actually playing it.

Just as the game was ending, Lars came running up to the five Owls with his news.

"Nish has been arrested!"

"What do you mean?" Travis asked. A hundred

images flashed through his mind – including, most prominently, Nish "flashing" some Russians as part of his stupid plan to get into *Guinness World Records* by mooning more people than anyone in history.

"You'll have to see for yourself," Lars said.

The group of Owls hurried around to the other side of the Ufa Arena. In an open area, they found a giant table-hockey game where fans could move the two life-size players by working large controls along the side.

Over in the corner, a group had gathered. Travis could tell from the distinctive fur hats with badges on them that several of the people were Russian police. Through a small opening in the circle of adults, he could also see Nish, standing in the middle with a policeman on either side of him, both of them with a solid grip on his arms.

Nish had his choirboy look on, but Travis didn't think he looked all that innocent.

Muck and Mr. D and Dmitri's dad were also there. Mr. Yakushev was in discussion with the police, and then he turned to translate for Muck and Mr. D.

"They say he climbed onto the game and started playing with a real stick while other kids were trying to play properly," Mr. Yakushev said.

"Apparently he even threw a hip check into one of the players."

One of the policemen pointed angrily at the giant table-top game, and everyone's eyes followed his finger. Travis saw instantly what the policeman meant. One of the forwards was badly bent, as if something large had crashed into it.

"Did you do that?" Mr. D asked Nish, who instantly turned red and beamed.

"He tripped me," Nish explained, with his choirboy smile.

"Not the time or the place for joking, young man," Muck said. "You should immediately apologize."

Nish winced. He hated apologizing almost as much as he hated vegetables.

"I'm sorry," he said in a very small voice.

"Speak up," Muck ordered. "I want everyone to hear you."

"I'm sorry," Nish said louder. "I'm sorry I hurt the game."

Mr. Yakushev translated Nish's words into Russian.

"Now tell them you will pay for any repairs," Muck told Nish.

Nish looked up as if he'd just taken a slap shot to the stomach. That was another thing about Nish. He hated spending money. And he never had any.

"Say it," Muck said.

"Okay," Nish said with a sullen look. "I'll pay for whatever needs to be done – but I have no money."

Mr. Yakushev translated for the police. Travis figured he'd left out the bit about Nish having no money.

The policeman nodded at his colleagues and they released their grip on Nish's arms.

The officer walked up to Nish, put his face right up to the young hockey player's, and bawled him out loudly in Russian for a full minute, then suddenly stopped, turned, and walked angrily away.

"Man," Nish said. "That is baaaaaad breath!"

"Just be thankful you have any breath of your own left in you, young man," said Muck. "This was even stupider than usual for you. Another trick like that, and you'll not only not be playing, you'll be on your way home."

Muck walked away as abruptly as the policeman had, and before long the crowd had all departed.

Nish blinked after them; only a small group of Owls were left now at the side of the giant table-top game.

"Can't anyone around here take a joke?"

Sam had had enough. "Don't you get it?" she said to him. "*You* are the joke."

12

Olga brought me a gift this morning. She was smiling again and very friendly. Too friendly. And why a gift? What is she expecting in return? I have nothing here but my pack. I have no money.

"Open," she kept saying. I didn't want to open any gift. Then I'd have to say thank you or something. Thanks for keeping me locked up away from my mother and father?

But she wouldn't leave until I opened it, so I gave a big sigh she couldn't possibly miss and I opened the bag she'd brought. I pulled out a wooden doll. It was mostly round and smooth and beautifully painted, a young girl with fair hair, a nice smile, and cheeks as red as a fire engine.

Olga said the doll looked like me. I couldn't really see that, but I did sort of like it – even if I stopped playing with dolls years ago.

"*Matryoshka*," Olga said several times until I was able to repeat it: "*ma-tree-oosh-ka*."

"That is name of doll," Olga said. "They are called *matryoshka*. I will show you."

Olga twisted the doll sharply so that it came apart in the middle. She pulled off the top. Inside the doll was another doll, exactly the same.

"Neat!" I said.

"Wait," she said. "There is more."

She pulled out the inside doll and twisted it apart, revealing yet another doll: exactly the same but smaller, so that it fit inside the other.

She did this five times until there were six identical dolls lined up, each one an exact copy of the other, except smaller. I put the smallest one back inside the second-smallest one, then that one back inside the third-smallest, until finally there was just the one again, so perfectly painted it seemed there could only be the one doll.

"It is yours," Olga said. "Gift from Olga to Sarah."

"*Spasiba*," I said to her. She had taught me the Russian word for thank you.

It seemed odd to be receiving a gift from your kidnapper, and even odder to be grateful for it, but everything about this experience is odd.

The doll – or dolls – remind me of that funny thing Muck said to our parents the evening we got together to talk about this trip. What was it again? Russia is a riddle or something, inside a mystery, wrapped in an . . . an . . . enigma. Yes, enigma. Something impossible to understand – sort of like Nish!

Olga said I should get ready for another work-out on the ice, so I did. I know I shouldn't feel this way, but I was glad for the chance to burn off some energy doing what I like to do best.

The two young men, Pavel and Sacha, were there again. Both had on the same socks and jerseys as Olga had given me to wear – all red, except for the golden two-headed eagle.

Sacha spoke very little English, but Pavel knew lots of English words. He was friendly – more so than Sacha. Pavel said we should run some more drills together.

That was fine with me. It's not much fun skating alone anyway. Once you've done the "alone" tricks – fire a puck off the crossbar, skate some crossover patterns, fool with the pucks – it quickly gets old.

We were warming up when the quieter guy, Sacha, skated over to me.

"Show me trick," he said.

I wasn't sure what he meant. So he pretended to be scooping the puck up the way I've been doing lately. He bent over, laid his stick flat on the ice, twirled it, and then held it out to me as if a puck were sitting on the blade.

But I was alone when I did that the other day. They had come out later.

They must have filmed me doing it. I guess Sacha saw it and was impressed.

We went over to where the other skater, Pavel, had dropped some pucks. The ice was still forming, and the pucks weren't frozen, so it was easy enough to do the trick. I got mine up first scoop, twirled, and handed it to Sacha.

He tried it several times with no luck. Pavel came over and began working on it, too. He almost succeeded on the first try, but the puck flew away when he tried the twirl move to bring the puck onto the surface of the blade.

I worked with them for a while. They were laughing at their mistakes, but soon they started to get the hang of it. Pavel picked one up perfectly and did a big whoop of triumph.

A whistle blew. Loud.

Standing on the players' bench, staring hard at us from under his hat, was the tall man I had seen watching me before.

He shouted out something in Russian. He seemed angry. Sacha and Pavel jumped at his orders. Pavel seemed especially upset.

We began running drills. They set up the first ones: breakout patterns, three-on-ones against a pylon – hardly tough to get around that! – and a few skating drills that involved turning at full speed once you hit the red line and skating backward at top speed until you crossed the blue lines. I could soon tell that I was better at that drill than the young men.

I didn't see the tall man again – thankfully! – but I was aware that the cameras were tracking us. You could sometimes even hear the whirr of a camera turning if you were close enough to the boards.

But why? What is the purpose of it all?

What is at the bottom of this *matryoshka* of a hockey prison?

13

Travis leaned back and strained to look down the bench, all the way to the far end, where the spare goalie sat during games.

Jenny was there in full equipment, gloves on, mask off, Screech Owls ball cap on her head, with her brown ponytail sticking out the back. Jeremy was in nets today for the Owls' match against Saint Petersburg, considered one of the tournament favorites to take the gold medal.

Normally, as the backup goaltender, Jenny would be the last Owl along the bench. But there was one more player sitting beyond her, one player seemingly separated from the rest of the team.

Nish.

Travis could see enough of the chubby Owls defenseman to know that Nish was in his "keep-out-the-world" position. His back was almost horizontal, meaning Nish was sitting with his head resting on his shin pads, his face staring directly down at his skates. Travis didn't have to see Nish's round face to know what color it would be.

It was a wonder there wasn't steam coming out Nish's ears. Muck had told him to "staple" his big butt there right after warm-up. He didn't need to explain. Nish was still in the coach's bad books. First it was the glory goal against Minsk, then the incident with the giant-sized table-hockey game. Muck was sending a tough message to their assistant captain.

Travis breathed deeply. The Owls *needed* Nish. The Saint Petersburg Pushkins were no *push*overs. They were well outfitted, well coached and extremely fast. Not only that, but they had a good feel for the larger ice surface, which the Owls had only played on a few times. Dmitri had helped explain the added importance of "cycling" pucks out of corners and the little bit of extra time defense had to get shots in from the point, but being told in the dressing room and putting it into practice on the ice were worlds apart.

The Owls could use Nish on defense. More significantly, they needed Sarah's speed up front. Andy was a good fill-in, but he wasn't the fastest skater, and so Travis's line – with Dmitri on the far wing – was struggling.

Muck had told them before the game that the Pushkins were named after a famous Russian poet. Travis thought a North American team named for a poet would be laughed off the ice, but the tough Russian side was up 3–0 before the Owls finally caught a break. It was Fahd, of all people, who broke up the middle with the puck. Fahd was the last Owl you'd expect to carry the puck – usually he was quick to dish off to whomever was closest to him – but it was almost as if little Fahd knew that if Nish wasn't there to lug the puck out of the Owls' end, he had better do so instead.

Travis moved in behind Fahd and tapped his stick twice, quickly, just to let him know he was there. Muck had told them no one was more disliked on a team than a player who hammered his stick endlessly on the ice to signal he was open and wanted a pass. If you wanted to tell a teammate you were open, Muck said, a quick tap would do.

Fahd dropped the puck as he went over the Saint Petersburg blue line, and Travis picked it up, curling over against the boards.

He saw Dmitri coming hard down the right side, but there was no clear lane for a safe pass.

Travis fired the puck hard instead, far ahead of Dmitri. It hit the far boards and spurted back, perfectly timed for Dmitri to pick it up in full flight.

The Owls had seen it a hundred times before: Dmitri using his speed on the outside to loop around the defense; Dmitri cutting back to the net, a shoulder deke, front-hand fake, backhand, roofer – the water bottle spinning high as the puck flew in just under the crossbar.

"I didn't know you could carry the puck like that," Travis said as he gently cuffed the back of Fahd's helmet.

Fahd was laughing. "Neither did I."

The Owls took it to 3–2 when Derek Dillinger managed to tip a Fahd shot – *Fahd again!* – from the point late in the second when the Owls got a power play after one of the Pushkins had tripped Jesse Highboy.

And they tied the game 3–3 halfway through the third when Willie Granger took a hard shot from the right circle that bounced off two different Pushkin defenders, looped high in the air, and somehow dropped onto the back of the Pushkin goaltender and dribbled into the net.

Five minutes left in the game. Muck walked to the far end of the bench. He passed right by Jenny and stood for a moment behind Nish, who was still sitting there with his face pressed hard between his knees.

Muck leaned over and touched Nish's shoulder.

He hadn't said a word. Nish hadn't looked back to ask. Both of them knew exactly what it meant.

Nish was over the boards in a flash, not even waiting for Jenny to open the gate, and was stretching and twisting as he moved down ice to take up his position for the face-off. Lars, the Owls' other best defenseman, was on the other side. Travis knew immediately Muck's strategy: go for it; put Nish out when he had something to prove.

Travis smiled to himself. It was a wonder that Nish didn't come with a bunch of buttons and switches down his front, because Sarah and Sam knew exactly what buttons to push to get him going or to bring him down. And Muck always knew which switch to flip when he needed something special from the goofy defenseman.

But that was Wayne Nishikawa, thought Travis. You couldn't have one side without the other. You got the total nutcase, the troublemaker, the goof one minute; and the next minute, you got the skilled hockey player with the heart of a lion.

Gordie Griffith took the face-off and managed to kick the puck back to Lars, who immediately skated back behind the Screech Owls' net – "Lars's Office" the Owls sometimes called it – and there he waited. A Pushkin forechecker swooped in to see if he could scare up a pass, but Lars calmly tapped the puck off the back boards and back to his own stick as the checker flew by.

Lars faked a pass to Jesse on the one side, and instead backhanded the puck over to Nish in the far corner. Nish began to rumble down the ice, lugging the puck as if it were taped to his stick.

Nish worked past all three forwards – then, just as he hit the blue line, he put the puck over to Gordie, who quickly rapped it off the boards back to Lars.

Lars took it as he crossed the blue line, then did his spinnerama move to elude one checker. He faked a shot, balked on the down-swing as a Pushkin defender went down to block the shot, and gently threw a saucer pass over the outstretched body of the checker that landed to the left of the net, right in Nish's wheelhouse.

Nish hammered home a slap shot that gave the goaltender no chance.

Owls 4, Saint Petersburg 3. Four goals in a row by the Owls to take the lead and only minutes left to play.

The Owls on the ice raced to congratulate Nish, who could normally be expected to throw his body against the glass or go down spinning on his knees and fake he was shooting an arrow into the net. But this time there was nothing.

Nothing.

Travis and Dmitri started laughing. Here was something brand-new: Humble Nish. Humble Nish lowered his head, gave no high-fives, no cheers, not even a smile. He returned to the bench as quietly as if he were returning a library book, and sat once again at the far end.

Travis couldn't resist. He turned to look back. Muck was staring at Mr. D, who was rolling his eyes.

Travis couldn't be certain, but he thought that Muck was stifling a laugh.

The Owls returned to the Astoria Hotel triumphant. They had beaten one of the tournament favorites 5–3 – Sam had scored in the final seconds into an empty net – and they must now be considered a favorite. And they had done it without Sarah Cuthbertson, their best player, and *almost* without Wayne Nishikawa, their top defenseman.

The parents also came along to the Astoria. Dmitri's father had said that there would be a meeting about Sarah. The police would be there. As would Mr. Petrov.

They gathered in the hotel lounge. Mr. Yakushev spoke, at times translating what he said into Russian for the benefit of the police.

"Sarah is safe and well," he announced, taking off his glasses as if, finally, he could relax his guard.

Travis felt such relief he thought he was going to burst into tears. Sam was already bawling.

"Sarah is safe, and we know for sure she is well and healthy. The police have received photographs of her and a video message. She says in the video that she is fine and is being treated well. It is exactly as the police suspected."

"But she's not here?"

"Not yet. The message also included a ransom request. I will ask Mr. Petrov to speak about that."

Mr. Petrov moved to the front. He was breathing hard, likely feeling the same flood of relief the Owls all felt. He smiled before he spoke. He only spoke a little English, and Mr. Yakushev helped him along.

"I consider this my responsibility," he told the players and parents, with Mr. Yakushev's assistance. "I am the one who brought you all, and Sarah, here to Ufa. And there can be no doubt the ransom is directed at me, not you. I am working with the police to negotiate a safe return for your teammate and your daughter. I can promise you, she will be returned safe and sound."

The parents spontaneously broke out in applause and cheers. Mr. Petrov smiled and seemed grateful to shake the hands offered by the parents.

"How much are they asking?" Fahd asked when he got close to Mr. Petrov. Leave it to Fahd to ask the awkward, as well as the obvious, question. Travis was glad he had.

Mr. Petrov swallowed, considering what to say. "They are looking for ten million rubles," he said quietly.

Mr. D whistled. The other parents seemed in shock. If he was willing to pay that much for her safe return, he was a very generous man. No way could Sarah's parents afford that, or even all the team's parents put together.

"How much is that?" Fahd asked later, when the Owls had returned to their rooms.

Data was already on his tablet, doing conversions.

"In American dollars," he announced, "it would be approximately $333,370, depending on the daily rate of exchange."

Sam sniffed. "Sarah's worth a lot more than that," she said.

Travis could not even imagine $333,000 – he had about $20 in his own bank account – but he had to agree.

Sarah was priceless to the Owls.

14

I was back on the ice this morning. It was very different.

Pavel and Sacha were there again, and so was the tall man in the hat — always standing far back, as if he didn't want to be seen up close.

What was different was me. Before I dressed to go out onto the ice, Olga took me into this room where there were people waiting around. They seemed to have more to do with science than hockey. They had me lie on a bed, and they taped tiny sensors all over my head. What were they looking for? Brainwaves? Escape plans?

They also taped sensors to my legs and arms. And finally they gave me a new hockey helmet. It was very different from the one I had been wearing. When I first tried it on, I thought it was too big – something a large man might wear – but then I saw it in the mirror and understood.

The helmet had a built-in camera.

Once all the sensors had been attached and double-checked to see if they were being picked up on the various computers around the room, they let me finish dressing to play hockey. Olga helped, because it wasn't easy pulling on socks, for example, over the sensors and wires that had been taped all over me.

I didn't feel right at first, but after a few laps around the rink, I sort of forgot that I was completely wired and began fooling around with the pucks. Pavel managed to do the scoop perfectly and we all laughed.

That felt very odd. Here we were, playing. I didn't know who they were. I wasn't there voluntarily.

I was their prisoner – well, if not their prisoner, then surely the prisoner of the tall man who was watching. They should have been my sworn enemies, and yet here we were, playing on the ice and laughing at each other trying my little scoop trick with the puck.

On the ice, they felt more like friends – especially Pavel. I wondered how they felt about me. They had to know that I was there against my wishes.

After we had warmed up and tried a few simple drills – I even taught them one of Muck's – the doors opened at the Zamboni end and a bunch of new players came out. As far as I could tell, all of them were girls. They said nothing to me.

Pavel said we were to play a scrimmage and that they wanted me to try my best, because it would be the three of us and a goaltender against a full team on the other side, two full lines of five apiece.

We wouldn't stand a chance.

I guess they knew me better than I know myself, though. My mother always says I'm hopelessly stubborn. According to her, I can never resist a challenge.

This was going to be an incredible challenge.

But it didn't take more than a couple of rushes by the three of us, or a few rushes by the other side, for me to see that it wasn't as impossible as it might have looked. The other players were good, but not quite as good as Pavel and Sacha.

And the three of us clicked. It may have been because of all the drills we had been doing, but it might as easily have been luck. Muck likes to say the "hockey gods" have control of the game. He says there is no way in the world that any hockey coach can map out plays the way football coaches can. Hockey has a magic to it that humans can't understand and should simply enjoy.

The three of us had that magic, just like Dmitri, Trav, and I have a bit of magic going for us. I always know where they'll be. I know how Travis likes to curl away and look for the play. I know how Dmitri will always use his speed to drive to the outside, and how, nine times out of ten, he'll try to roof the puck on the backhand, which goalies never seem to expect.

Pavel has superb speed – sort of like Dmitri. And Sacha sees the ice unbelievably. I like to think that is my gift, too – I can see where the players are without really looking hard, and I can guess where the puck is going to go in the next few seconds. My dad once made me a sign for my bedroom wall and told me it was a quote from Wayne Gretzky: "Skate to where the puck is going to be, not to where it has been."

Anyway, we worked well together. I even looped one of those high Lars passes down ice, and Pavel sensed the play perfectly. He flew by the other side's defense and picked up the puck just as it slapped back down on the ice. He scored easily.

It was tough, playing three skaters on five. I had to protect the puck a lot by keeping it in my skates when there was heavy traffic. I'm good at this, so we were often able to work a puck along the boards, me keeping it while Pavel slipped out into the slot, where I could feed him for a one-timer.

We played first-to-ten wins, and we won 10–7. After I put in the tenth goal, I could hardly catch my breath.

I was sweating heavily. I started laughing to myself, thinking the salty sweat might short-circuit the sensors.

Actually, I had forgotten all about them. The reason was, I have to admit, I was having fun.

15

"No word?"

Travis must have asked this same question a dozen times since they heard that Sarah was safe and a ransom had been demanded.

Sam was philosophical. "I imagine they're bargaining about the price," she said. "Mr. Petrov said he'd pay, but even for him ten million rubles isn't chicken feed."

"I bet they're setting a trap," Data butted in. "They're planning one. I can practically guarantee it. It's how they catch blackmailers all the time. They might be marking the money up so that it colors their hands when they touch it. They might be planning a drop somewhere where they can have the area completely surrounded by hidden cops."

"You watch too much TV," said Lars.

"What do you expect me to do – snowboard?"

Travis cringed. It was unusual for Data to snap at someone like that. He had never acted sorry for himself. Data had always tried to make the best of everything – after that drunk driver had hit him, he'd stayed with the team, and Muck and Mr. D had made him an assistant coach.

Data's making a sarcastic crack like that showed how on edge the Owls still were about Sarah. How nervous they were despite all the assurances that Sarah was just fine and would be back with the Screech Owls as soon as a ransom could be arranged.

"When's our next game?" Nish asked.

"It's also our last game," added Lars.

"Tonight at seven thirty," said Sam. "We're up against some place I can't even pronounce."

"Yekaterinburg," Data said impatiently. "It's the fourth-largest city in Russia and has a population of one and a half million. It's not far from here."

"Someone said they're better than Saint Petersburg," said Fahd.

"So?" said Sam. "We already proved *we're* better than Saint Petersburg. This one's for the championship."

Travis felt his inner captain stirring. He had to give his teammates some new focus. He had to stop the sarcasm and the fretting and the useless chatter.

Perhaps it would help if they weren't all just sitting around in the lobby. Muck had said that if they stayed together in groups of at least four, then they were free to walk about the city in daylight.

"You know everything about Ufa, Data. What can we go see?"

Data listed some attractions off the top of his head: statues, parks, the theater, ballet. They weren't so interested in any of those. He told them that Ufa's pro hockey team, Salavat Yulaev, was back in town and practicing this week.

Nish looked disgusted. "What's Saliva Yuck – some sort of *snot*?"

Data was really peeved now. "Salavat Yulaev, idiot. The team is named after a great national hero."

Data's fingers danced over his tablet as he googled the team name.

"He lived about two hundred and fifty years ago," he told them. "He was a freedom fighter – a revolutionary – and he died in prison. There's a big statue to him here, and it has one of his poems on it."

Data read the English translation: "I would return home, but alas, / I am in chains . . ."

"Sounds like Sarah," Sam said. Nish giggled. No one else laughed.

Data continued: "The road home may be obscured by snow, / But come spring it shall melt – / I am not dead yet, my Bashkirs!"

"What's a Bashkir?" Fahd asked.

"The people here are Bashkir," Data explained. "Ufa is in the Republic of Bashkortostan – it used to be its own country."

"I'm just happy to hear the snow will melt," Nish said. He had already lost interest in Data's history lesson.

"Where do you think the team would be practicing?" Lars said suddenly. "The peewee tournament has taken over the new rink."

Data, still seeming a bit testy, began typing on his tablet. He hunted around on Google until he had an address for an older downtown rink.

"This will be it," he said. "Seats about four thousand. Banners are still hanging there, apparently, from the team's championship run."

"We should check it out," Travis said. It would give them something to do. Give the Owls something to think about other than Sarah.

"I'll ask at the front desk for a map," said Lars.

"No need," Data said. "I downloaded an app for Russian maps onto my phone."

Data switched from his tablet to his mobile, waited while the phone app picked up a signal, and then held out the phone so the rest of the Owls could see the screen.

Travis could make out streets and some landmarks. He could see the large park beside the Ufa Arena, and the shopping mall. There was also a red squiggly line running from a spot on Karl Marx Street away from the arena where they were playing. It was the route to the downtown rink.

Data examined it carefully. "Looks like about ten or twelve blocks, easily walkable."

"Let's go check it out," said Sam.

"Can we borrow your phone?" Fahd asked Data.

Data was reluctant to give it up, but he knew they'd never find the old rink on their own.

"Guard it with your *life*!" Data snapped as he practically tossed it at him.

Travis suddenly understood. Data was feeling left out. It was almost impossible to get around in a wheelchair in Ufa. Even with his power wheels, Data couldn't navigate the unplowed streets. And once he got to wherever it was the Owls were going, there was no guarantee he'd be able to get in. It was fortunate for him that the new rink was modern and had some provisions for wheelchairs and scooters.

"We will," Fahd said, putting the phone in the pocket of his Screech Owls hoodie. "Promise."

16

It was good to get out walking. There was light snow falling, which seemed to happen every day in Ufa. It must have snowed harder during the night, as the side streets were thick with snow and had yet to be plowed. They laughed at a couple of young women trying to make their way down one of the snowed-in streets in high-heeled boots.

"Maybe they get better traction," suggested Sam. "Sort of like ski poles."

The five Screech Owls giggled as they passed the young women, and Travis felt good hearing the familiar sounds of his best friends. There hadn't been enough laughter on this trip. Not even Nish had been able to break the feeling of tension since Sarah had disappeared.

With Fahd calling out directions from the GPS on Data's phone, they worked their way along Lenin Street, where front-end loaders were already dumping snow onto trucks to be hauled away. There was much activity in the streets: blue Christmas lights still burning into the daylight, bundled-up shoppers making their way along the cleared sidewalks, cars and trucks moving so fast and in such numbers along the main road that the Owls could only cross at lights – and even then they had to hurry.

But the air was cold and fresh and the store windows fascinating. They passed flower shops and high fashion stores and small grocery stores and entrances to malls that had been built inside ancient buildings. They marveled at the number of people – women as well as men – smoking cigarettes as they walked along.

"They obviously *encourage* smoking here," said Nish. "I'm gonna buy a pack."

"Do, and we'll butt you off the team," said Sam. Nish delivered one of his beloved tongue-out raspberries and the others laughed.

Travis had been right. The distraction was good for the Owls. They had somewhere to go and things to see – and for the most part they weren't dwelling on their missing teammate and friend.

"It's just off this street coming up," said Sam, checking the phone.

The five Screech Owls turned as a group: Travis, Sam, Lars, Fahd, and, bringing up the rear, Nish.

"*There it is!*" Fahd shouted, pointing triumphantly.

They had come to a small park with play structures underneath the snow, and beyond that a large gray building that looked more like an abandoned factory than a hockey rink. But an abandoned factory would have its windows all broken; this building seemed to have no windows at all.

"It's as ugly as Nish's butt," said Sam.

"You're sure this is the right place?" Travis asked.

Sam checked the map again and nodded. "This is it."

They walked around to the other side and found the entrance. There was a sign in Russian, as well as a symbol of someone skating. It was indeed a rink.

Nish walked right up to the front door and yanked on the handle – but the door wouldn't budge. He tried again, but still it wouldn't open. Lars tried the door beside it, and it, too, would not budge.

"*Locked!*" said Lars.

"But there's got to be people inside," Sam said. "Look."

She pointed to a parking area over to one side. There were several cars there. All the windshields were cleared of snow, so the vehicles had to have been driven there that morning, after the big snowfall.

They walked down to a side entrance, but it, too, was locked. It looked as if they weren't going to see Salavat Yulaev practice after all.

"We're beaten," Lars said with a disappointed sigh.

"No we're not," said Nish.

All eyes turned and stared at him. The last Screech Owl any of them expected to figure things out was big No. 44, Wayne Nishikawa.

"Follow me."

17

What was it Alice said when she found herself in Wonderland? "Curiouser and curiouser"?

That's pretty much how all of this seems to me. Everything up is down, everything down is up. Nothing makes sense. I'm a captive, but I'm treated well. I've been taken from my hockey team, but I'm playing hockey.

The games are fun, but sometimes I'm so wired up with sensors that I can feel them when I go full stride. Still, it's not bad. I've gotten to quite like horsing around on the ice with Pavel and Sacha. Especially Pavel. I feel he could have been a real friend if we had met somewhere that wasn't half rink, half prison.

I wonder what their role is in this whole thing. They sure don't seem the kind of people who would ever want to hurt anyone. They seem nice – typical hockey players who just want to have fun.

I'm not allowed to talk to the girls who come out, but that's hardly a problem – I don't speak Russian, and they don't seem to speak any English. They treat me like I'm some sort of superstar, and I sometimes see them trying my moves. I like it, I have to admit. It's sort of flattering.

Olga said that today I'm to head for the ice and bring along my tracksuit and sneakers for some tests they want to run immediately after the on-ice workout with the team. So I've put on my hockey equipment already – everything except my skates – and I've got my tracksuit in my pack.

I hope this is over soon. Sometimes, when I'm too upset to sleep, I think they are being nice to me just so I will cooperate. But what happens when they have no more use for me?

It's not just curiouser and curiouser – I'm frightened.

18

"This way!" Nish hissed at the Owls following him around to the back of the old arena.

He stopped at the corner and peered around slowly, as if expecting to get blasted in the face by snowballs. Nish was in full "spy" mode – Wayne Nishikawa, Special Agent 44.

"What the heck are you doing?" Sam growled, clearly unimpressed.

"Shh!" he said, looking back, a finger pressed to his lips.

"What are we doing?" Travis asked.

Nish turned around. He was sweating. It was very cold outside, but he was still sweating.

"The Zamboni has to come out to dump after a flood," said Nish. "We all know that from the rink back home. Once that big door goes up, we slip in."

"We'll get caught," protested Fahd. He sounded scared.

"The door is likely automatic," said Nish. "It'll be just the one guy driving the Zamboni, and he has to concentrate on where he's going to dump it. You can see where they put it, over there."

Nish pointed to a large snow pile. They could see the tire marks from the Zamboni – heavy treads so it could grip on the ice – and it seemed the machine had made several trips to dump its scraped-up snow already that day. The arena ice was not as pure white as the freshly fallen snow. And it looked as if it were packed more tightly.

"We wait," said Nish, acting as if he were fully in charge.

"And then what?" asked a skeptical Sam.

"And then we go in and watch some truly amazing pro-level Russian hockey," said Nish, as if it were the most obvious thing in the world.

"There!"

Too late, Travis realized he had shouted this out.

He had been staring at the falling snowflakes, big fat flakes falling so slowly it seemed they had parachutes. They were hypnotic. Travis and the others had taken turns trying to catch them on their tongues.

But now the garage-style door was opening. Automatically, just as Nish had said it would.

The door rose slowly, creaking, the sound of the chain pulling it loud in the quiet lot where the Owls were hidden, waiting.

With a roar, the Zamboni made its exit from the rink. It moved slowly as it followed the familiar trail to where it dumped its contents.

The Owls waited until the driver had begun working the gears to release the snow carried in the Zamboni's belly, then darted for the open door.

No one said a word. They slipped in the door and quickly checked to see if there was another worker anywhere around. At the arena back home, they always worked in twos: one to drive the machine, one to move the nets aside and replace them, then shovel off the snow that the machine always dropped as it left the ice. When the second worker closed the doors through which the Zamboni had exited the ice, that was the sign it was now okay for the skaters to come back on.

Travis had sometimes wondered how much time he had lost in his life watching Zambonis circle the ice, how much time he'd spent waiting for those doors to slam shut so he could skate out onto the freshly flooded ice. If hockey players could get back their "Zamboni time" at the end of their lives, he figured it would add up to several years.

But here no one else was around. The Zamboni driver must have been working alone. They slipped along the boards closest to them, where the stands were only three rows deep. They kept low, their heads well below the top of the boards, just in case anyone was on the ice, though they could hear no sounds of skates.

As soon as Nish came to the first break in the stands, he ducked in under. The others followed suit, each player being high-fived by Nish as they passed by him. They were safe.

They couldn't stop giggling about their little trick on the Zamboni driver, but Travis was quick to hold a finger to his lips and call for silence. In the empty rink, any sound they made would carry. They caught their breath and waited until they could hear the Zamboni come back into the chute area and stop. Then they heard the big door to the outside close. And a few minutes after that, they could hear the first light sizzle of skates on ice. The practice was on!

Led by Nish and Sam, the Owls moved back and climbed up behind the rear of the stands. It allowed them to look down from under the seats and still be unseen.

The Screech Owls groaned quietly as one. This wasn't the big Russian team. There were *girls* all over the ice, and two young men who seemed like coaches. The girls were all wearing the same uniform – bright red with a sharp yellow crest that looked, to Travis, like some sort of fierce bird with two heads.

"That's the Russian team crest," said Fahd.

"How do you know?" asked Sam.

"They have it on caps at the souvenir stand," Fahd answered. "Didn't you see?"

"I did," said Lars. "I saw them."

The ice was still slick. The two men – both wearing red tracksuits with the yellow bird crest – went to the bench and yanked two pails of pucks up from the seats and dumped them out onto the ice. Some of the pucks bounced, some rolled, some slapped flat and seemed to freeze to the ice.

Travis watched one of the girls – a player he had already thought was the best skater of the bunch – skate over to the pucks and place the back of her stick blade on top of one of the pucks; then she scooped the puck and twirled.

Travis thought he was going to have a heart attack.

"That's –" he started to say.

"I know," Sam said, cutting him off. "That's *Sarah's* move!"

19

The Owls scrambled down from the stands and huddled at the bottom. They spoke in whispers, careful not to be heard or seen.

"What's going on here?" Sam wanted to know.

"Only Sarah does that move," Travis said.

"I can do it," said Nish. Sam looked hard at him, as if jamming an imaginary cork into his big mouth.

"How would *they* learn it?" Lars asked.

"They must have seen Sarah do it," said Sam. "That means she could be here somewhere."

Nish looked up briefly, his face now serious. He climbed up the back of the stands again, then came back down, shaking his head. "She's not on the ice."

"Where would she be?" asked Fahd.

"We're going to have to look around," said Travis. "Fahd and Lars, you stay here. Nish and Sam, go that way. I'll go this way. Stay down, just see what we can see."

"I don't want to stay," protested Fahd.

Travis tapped the phone Fahd still held in his hand. "You've got this. If something goes wrong, use it."

"Call nine-one-one?" Fahd asked.

"They might not have nine-one-one here," said Travis. "Call the hotel and ask them to put you through to Data's room. He put the number in before we left."

Nish and Sam were already on their way, moving silently beneath the stands. Travis doubled back toward the Zamboni chute and then turned through the first exit from the ice surface.

There was a door, with a handle, but this time when he turned it, the door opened. He was through.

Travis found himself in a long corridor. There were rubber mats laid down to protect people's skates, so the corridor must lead to dressing rooms. He moved quickly, darting ahead when he was sure he couldn't be seen, slipping behind support columns and garbage bins and rows of lockers when he got nervous.

He could see a row of windows ahead that looked into another room. The room was much more brightly lit than the corridor, so he crouched extra low and made his way toward it, crawling in between the wall and a support column. For one of the few times in his life, Travis was glad he was small. He fit the narrow space. No one could see him if they walked by. And if he stretched himself high, he'd be able to see in one of the windows.

Travis slowly counted to ten to try and calm himself. He breathed in and out, deliberately slowing his breath. He was sure he had a grip on himself now.

He stretched to look.

He saw a bank of computers with people in white lab coats working at several of them. He saw some workout machines: treadmills, spinning bikes, weight machines, step machines.

And then he saw Sarah! She was wearing one of the red tracksuits with the yellow bird crest. She was doing sprints on a treadmill, and she seemed to have a dozen wires running off her body. There were wires attached to her legs, her arms, her chest, her neck – and even four to her head. She was running easily. On either side of her stood one of the white-coated people, a woman on her right, a man on her left. They held stopwatches and clipboards.

Travis dropped back down. His heart was pounding.

He had found Sarah.

She was alive and well and, he had to admit, didn't seem particularly unhappy. That would be Sarah, though. If Nish was the Owl who hated practice and exercise most of all, Sarah would be the one who most enjoyed it. Workouts were like oxygen to her. She craved them.

He had to tell the others. He had to slip back the way he had come. And he had to do it unseen.

Back through the long corridor Travis snaked, moving quickly from hiding spot to hiding spot.

This time, instead of slipping behind the lockers, he dashed across in front of them.

And when he did, he saw something.

It was only a flash out of the corner of his eye – something pink. But the color seemed as familiar as his own face.

He stopped behind a column and looked back. Several of the lockers were open. The girls' team seemed to be the only ones using the rink, and they must have felt secure enough to use the lockers without locking them. Several of them hadn't even bothered to close the doors.

And there, at one end, was the backpack Sarah had been wearing when she'd been kidnapped that day in the park.

Travis's first thought was to leave a note, but he had no paper, no pen. He could take something from the pack, but what would be the point of that? Sarah wouldn't take it as a sign. She'd think one of the Russian girls had stolen from her.

Reluctantly, Travis moved on, slipping carefully down the long corridor until he came to the exit back into the rink. He checked for anyone on the other side, turned the handle, stepped through, and slipped in under the stands, then made his way back to where the Owls had been.

Sam and Nish were already back.

"Anything?" Sam whispered as Travis made his way into their little hiding place. "We found nothing."

"I found her!" Travis said, trying to suppress his excitement.

Sam screeched and instantly clapped her hand over her mouth.

"Where?" asked Fahd.

"There's some laboratory set up in another part of the rink," Travis said. "They're doing tests on her. She's okay, though."

"You spoke to her?" asked Fahd.

"No, of course not – just saw her. She looked okay."

"We've got to get her out of here," said Sam.

"Can we tackle the guys who've got her?" Nish asked.

Travis looked at Nish and shook his head. "This isn't a movie, Nish. It's real. We can't risk her getting hurt."

"How do we tell her we know she's here?" asked Lars.

"If we could only get a message to her," said Sam.

Travis shook his head. Then he had an idea.

"I know," he said.

"What?" the other Owls all said at once.

"Fahd, give me the phone."

Fahd recoiled. "I can't. Data'd kill me."

"Give me the phone," Travis repeated. "This is much more important."

"More important than me getting killed?" Fahd said, looking shocked.

"You can't *phone* her," Nish said.

"I'll leave her the phone," Travis explained. "I saw her pack. I know where it is."

"But she might not be able to phone us," said Sam. "They could hear her. They probably have a guard on her at all times."

"She can text," Travis said. "And we can text her."

"How?"

"Jenny has her phone," Travis explained. "She won't turn it on because the charges would be so high, but we can help pay."

"Let's do it!" Sam almost shrieked.

"Data's phone," Travis ordered, holding out his hand toward Fahd.

Fahd looked as if he might cry. He hesitated, then slowly handed it over.

Travis grabbed it and immediately headed for the locker area and Sarah's backpack.

He'd hide it in the pack. She'd find it.

Wouldn't she?

20

Now I know what a laboratory rat feels like. I've been prodded, poked, measured, wired-up, tested, and examined so much I bet they have enough information to build a brand-new Sarah Cuthbertson out of titanium.

Hey, you don't suppose?

No, I can't see that. It would be some sort of Sarah Zombie. That's for science fiction movies, not peewee hockey teams.

I have some sense of what they're doing. Why

me, I don't know, but it has to be measuring how quickly I recover from exercise and how I move around the ice. Maybe the little attachments to my brain and that camera in my helmet have something to do with how I see the ice. I don't know. I'm getting sick of this. I want to see my mom and dad and the team – but there's not much I can do about it. I can't stomp my feet and yell and scream until they let me go.

But that's the point, isn't it? When will they let me go? And how will they let me go? They're very sophisticated, with their science and their tests, so they can't be so foolish as to think what they did is all right. They must be pretty confident that they can drop me off as safely as they grabbed me in the first place. And they must be pretty sure that I won't be able to tell the police anything about them.

I could describe Olga, but she's hardly the brains behind this. I could identify some of the researchers – and Sacha and Pavel – but they aren't behind it, either. Certainly not Pavel – he seems like he couldn't hurt a fly.

I just wish I could get a better look at that tall man who comes and stands at the back of the benches some days. He's got to be a big shot. Has to be.

Olga says that . . .

That was weird! My pen ran dry, so I dug down in the side pocket of my pack for another one. I knew I had a couple in there. But there was something else. A cell phone!

I couldn't believe it. I don't own a phone, even though I keep asking for one for my birthday. And I knew for sure there was nothing there before.

I thought maybe Olga put it there. At first her friendliness seemed fake, but now I think it's her real personality. In a weird way, she's a *nice* kidnapper. She knows I get bored, so maybe she was just giving me something to play games on.

I turned it on and it lit up! I figured the battery would be run down.

It took a moment for the screen to come into focus, but when it did, I could not believe what I was staring at: the Screech Owls' crest!

21

"Data's gonna kill me!" Fahd kept whining as the Owls made their way back to the hotel.

"If he doesn't, I will!" barked Sam, who was trying to get everyone to move as fast as possible. "Stop your whining and let's get back!"

They worked their way through backstreets and along main thoroughfares – at times losing their way now that they no longer had Data's phone. Travis was the one who recognized the tall, blue-gray building in the distance and knew the Hotel Astoria was just beyond it.

They burst into the lobby, ran past the hotel reception desk, and took the stairs rather than wait for the slow elevator. They had to get to Jenny's room, and fast.

Up the stairs they bounded, Sam and Travis in front, Lars and Fahd right behind, then big Nish huffing and puffing, his face the color of the Russians' tracksuits.

Jenny was reading. She'd been wondering where the others had gone off to, and Sam tried to tell her in as few words as she could: "We know where Sarah is. We need your phone. *Quick!*"

Jenny seemed stunned by the sudden arrival of the excited Owls. "I'm not using my phone over here," she said, not moving.

"*Get it!*" Sam shouted. "We left Data's phone for her to find –"

Just then, Data rolled in from the doorway. He'd heard his name.

"You left *what*?" he demanded.

"Your phone," Travis said.

"Sorry!" Fahd gulped. "I –"

But Data was glaring at Travis, waiting for an explanation.

"We know where Sarah is," he said quickly. "We were able to slip your phone to her."

"What's she gonna do?" asked Data. "Phone the police? You remember what Dmitri's dad said about the police – you can't always trust them. Maybe they're even in on it!"

"I doubt that," Sam said. "But if she phoned anyone, she would have to talk – and how do we know there isn't a microphone in the room where they're keeping her?"

"She can text," Travis said. "We can work a plan out. No one will know. We know how to get into the place where they're keeping her – it's a hockey rink!"

Data seemed skeptical. He turned on Fahd. "You lose my phone, you get me a new one."

"I will," said Fahd.

"*Data!*" Sam yelled. She grabbed him by the shoulders and shook hard. "It's *Sarah!* Don't you understand?"

Instantly, Data seemed to. Sam was so wound up she was crying.

"Jenny, we need that phone," Data said, putting his hand out.

Data took over. He turned on the phone and looked at the messages.

"Sarah's found it," he said. "We have a message."

"Read it! Read it!" Sam shouted.

"Jenny! It's me, Sarah," he read. "You're the only one with a phone, apart from Data, and I think this is his – but I have no idea how it got here."

Data's fingers flew as he texted back. He waited. The phone gave a light *ping*.

Data read: "I am kept in a room to the back of the 'lab' – directly opposite the ice surface . . ."

"I think I know where she means," said Travis.

"No one has hurt me. A woman, Olga, is trying to be nice to me, and so are the two hockey guys, Sacha and Pavel. I am left alone in the evenings after practice. I have to go. I'm expected back on the rink in five."

Data's fingers flew.

"What did you tell her?" asked Fahd.

"I said, 'Go.'"

"That's two letters," Fahd pointed out. "You typed more than that."

Data swallowed. "I told her we're coming to get her."

22

I thought my heart was going to pound right through my chest! I knew it was Data's phone the second I saw the Owls' logo, but I also knew it couldn't have been Data who put it there. Who, though? Trav? Sam? Dmitri? Maybe Dmitri – he's the only one who could talk his way in here. Not Nish. Definitely not Nish.

What to do, though? I have to confess to the silliest thing imaginable. My first thought was to check my e-mail! Once that ridiculous notion got out of my head, I began to think about what the phone meant and what I should do.

Whoever put it here – I'll bet Trav – would realize I'm being watched and can't risk making a call. And apart from the Owls, who could I call? I don't speak the language. So I would need to text someone. But who?

I went through the Owls one by one. Dmitri, no. Travis, no. Nish, no – certainly not Nish! Sam, no. Jenny . . . yes, Jenny! She has a phone, but she hasn't been using it. Too expensive, she said.

Still, the other Owls would also know she has a phone. They might have talked her into checking. So I sent a quick text and got an almost instant answer.

It came from Data. Data sending a text message to his own phone! But it meant that someone in the Owls had the team organized. Probably Trav. He'd be using Data as the communications expert, which he is.

I exchanged a few messages but then had to bail. I have an on-ice session coming up and have to get back in my hockey gear.

I made a decision while dressing. Maybe it's a stupid one, maybe not, but I'm going to do it.

I've put on my tightest T-shirt and tucked it in and done my hockey pants up as tightly as possible. I slipped Data's phone down the neck and let it drop so it rested against my stomach. I then put on a body shirt and tucked it in tight.

With my pants done up and my jersey hanging loose, no one can see.

I didn't do this so I can get a call or anything. I have another reason.

I just hope I don't mess up.

23

"We should get Muck and Mr. D," Fahd said.

Data shook his head. "Can't," he said. "They're not here. There's a big meeting over at the parents' hotel this afternoon. People from the Canadian embassy have flown in from Moscow to see if they can be of any help with Sarah. It's just the Owls here, no one else."

"We'll have to wait," Fahd said.

"No," Travis said. He surprised himself. He was really taking charge. He was the Screech Owls' captain and he was *acting* like the captain – especially with Sarah not here to help. "We're going to the rink to see if we can get her out."

"Muck won't like it," said Fahd.

"He'll like it fine if we get her safe and sound."

"I'll get Dmitri," said Sam. Travis nodded. They would need Dmitri. After all, he spoke the language.

There were seven of them: Travis, Sam, Nish, Lars, Fahd, Jenny – and now Dmitri. Once everyone was dressed and ready, they gathered in the lobby. They formed a quick circle and bumped fists together. A pact. A vow. Just like the Three Musketeers, except they numbered seven.

"All for one and one for all," said Fahd, who couldn't resist.

Sam corrected him. "All for Sarah."

"All for Sarah!" everyone said at once.

Data had downloaded the maps app onto Jenny's phone before they left, so the way back to the old rink seemed quick and easy. They were soon heading down the final street.

They decided on a game plan. Two of them – Jenny and Fahd – would stay outside and watch. They had no idea what they would do if something went wrong, but they'd at least be able to run back to the Astoria and let Muck and Mr. D know. The rest of them would head around the building to the back.

They waited patiently for the garage door to rise and didn't move until the Zamboni driver had headed out to dump his load of snow. They knew the ropes now, and were soon inside and hidden from sight underneath the stands.

They duck-waddled and dog-walked below the stands until they reached the place where they had previously gathered. Nish was first to climb up the back of the stands and stare out onto the ice surface.

"She's on," he said.

"Huh?" said Sam.

"Sarah," he said. "She's on the ice."

They all carefully climbed up and peered out. There was Sarah, all decked out in her Russian hockey equipment, showing one of the girls how to scoop a puck off the wet ice. She was laughing. She looked great.

"Maybe she's a traitor now," Nish suggested. "Gone over to the other side."

Dmitri hissed angrily. "Russia isn't *the other side*. It's not a communist country anymore. That's ancient history. We have criminals in Russia just the same as North America. Get real."

Nish burned red. "I was just joking."

"Okay," said Dmitri. "But don't forget that you and I are on the same team, right?"

Nish nodded, not sure what to say. He'd never seen Dmitri so angry.

"What are we going to do?" Sam asked.

They sat down and kicked around ideas. They could try and grab Sarah before she reached the room where they kept her, but there would be people around. Lots of people. The girl players. The two coaches. The men and women who ran the machines and the computers.

"We will have to wait until she's in her room," said Travis. "We'll wait for practice to end, and then, when the Zamboni is out, we'll make our way to the back. I'm pretty sure I know where her room is."

"How will we get in?"

"We have to hope there's a lock or a latch we can open on the outside."

"How long do we wait?" Lars asked.

"Long as it takes, I guess," Travis said.

"I have to go pee," said Nish.

The others turned and stared daggers at him.

"That's it," Travis said as he ducked back down under the stands. "They're headed off."

Hidden in the dark behind the stands, the Owls peered into the bright arena in front of them.

"The phone," Travis said. He took Jenny's phone and sent a text message to Sarah: "We are in the building. Be ready to go. Trav."

Sarah and the players left the ice, and shortly after, the Owls heard the Zamboni burp as it was started up. The driver opened up the doors onto the ice and soon came out on the Zamboni. The big machine chugged down the boards closest to where the Owls were hidden. Once it passed and the driver's back was to them, Travis moved into action.

He led them down, crouching and scrambling, until they reached the exit door he had found the last time. He waited, then moved quickly to slip through it. The others followed.

They waited briefly until the last of the Russian hockey players had cleared out of the locker area. Sarah was already gone. She had always been the fastest of the Owls to dress or change. Travis just hoped she was back in her room.

Once the way was clear, Travis told Sam, Lars, and Nish to wait where they were while he and Dmitri headed toward the back of the building.

He knew the way; Dmitri knew the language. They just hoped Dmitri wouldn't have to use it.

Travis and Dmitri bent low to get past the windows looking into the room with the machines and computers. There didn't seem to be anyone there. It was late afternoon. Perhaps they had all gone for the day.

Soon Travis was in an area he didn't know. He let himself be guided by instinct. He came to one corridor, passed by it, and moved on to the next. It was as far back in the building as they could go.

He peered down the corridor and saw several doors. One had light leaking out from below it.

Without saying a word, Travis pointed and indicated to Dmitri that this would be the room they would try.

They moved fast down the hall, still staying low, ready to bolt at any time.

Travis was first to the door. How, he wondered, had the pounding of his heart not set off the alarms? It sounded like a marching band, his heart like the big drums the marchers wore on their chests.

Dmitri was right beside him.

They examined the door. It had a latch on the outside, just as Travis had hoped.

He turned the handle slowly, then opened the door.

The bright light blinded them a bit. Travis blinked, stared. He was looking at one of the two young men who had been coaching Sarah.

The man said something in Russian. Travis knew it wasn't "Welcome! Come on in."

24

There was a message on the phone when I returned to my room and got out of my hockey equipment. It was Travis. He said they are in the building. Now all I can do is wait – and try to remember to breathe.

I'm so scared and nervous. I may as well scribble while I wait, or else I'll go mad.

I thought I heard a door click, but I can't look out to check. Still, I'm sure I heard something.

Didn't I?

25

Travis tried to speak, but some other foreign language – not Russian, not English – came babbling out. Dmitri brushed past him and stood between Travis and the Russian coach.

This was a Dmitri that Travis didn't know. Always so shy and soft-spoken back home, here he was being firm and confident and talking fast. Travis just had no idea what was being said.

The young Russian coach talked back. He

seemed angry at first, then thoughtful. More and more, the talking was being done by Dmitri.

Finally, the Russian coach nodded hard, stood up, and walked over.

Travis thought he was going to be hit. Or Dmitri was going to be slapped. At the very least, they were now going to be captured as well.

The coach said something in Russian.

Dmitri turned to Travis. "His name is Pavel. We're to go with him."

Travis's heart sank. They were caught.

With sagging shoulders, Travis followed Pavel and Dmitri down the hall. All the Screech Owls had managed to do was create more trouble. If the ransom was ten million rubles for Sarah alone, it would now be thirty million. And if the others were caught, seventy million.

Not even Mr. Petrov had that kind of money.

They came to an office-like room. Pavel reached inside the door and unhooked a bunch of keys from their place on the wall. He turned, jangling the keys.

We're going to be locked up, Travis thought. *Put in prison.*

They left the office and made their way along a short corridor. Here was a room where no light leaked out. A prison cell, thought Travis. A dungeon.

Pavel stopped, inserted the key, and turned it. He swung the door outward and stepped back so that Dmitri and Travis could enter.

Travis was crying as he stepped through. He couldn't help it. His eyes were streaming salty tears.

The light blurred in his tears. There was someone sitting on the side of a bed.

It was a girl. She had a Screech Owls coat on – and a pink backpack.

It was Sarah.

"Trav!" Sarah shouted. "Dmitri!"

She jumped off the bed and hugged Travis so hard he thought his chest was going to explode. He couldn't believe it. He hadn't seen her in days. At moments, he'd thought he might never see her again. But here she was. All ready to go – just as he had asked her to be. Now, all three of them would be locked up together.

"How did you get in?" Sarah asked, still not understanding. "How'd you get the key?"

Dmitri, who had said nothing, merely stood to one side and pointed out the doorway.

Pavel stood there, looking in, his face crumpling. He said something in Russian, and Dmitri explained that they were to follow him.

For a moment, Travis thought he had misheard. *Pavel was going to show them the way out.*

The three Screech Owls – Sarah with her backpack, Travis, then Dmitri – hurried along behind Pavel as he led them in another direction, looping around through a large storage area in the old rink, and then back through a door that took them to the spot where Sam and Nish and Lars were waiting.

The three waiting Owls looked shocked to see the group coming from the other direction. They, too, thought they'd been caught.

Pavel said something to Dmitri, and Dmitri answered him. Pavel nodded, backing away. They knew their own way from here.

"Pavel," Sarah said quickly. "Wait."

She walked back toward Pavel, who looked as if he was expecting to be slapped. But Sarah had no such intention.

She threw her arms around him and hugged him.

"*Spasiba*," she said. Thank you. "*Spasiba, Pavel.*"

26

The Owls came racing back to the Astoria just as Muck and Mr. D were arriving back from meeting with the embassy officials at the parents' hotel.

"SARAH!" Mr. D bellowed the moment he caught sight of her.

She raced to the Owls' manager and leaped into his arms for a huge bear hug.

Muck hugged her, too. The Screech Owls' coach was always awkward with emotion, but Travis could see the relief in his face and, for that matter, the tears in his eyes. Sarah was back. The world was all right again.

"That was fast work," Muck said. "Mr. Petrov just announced that the ransom had been paid. Did they drop you off here?"

"No," said Sarah.

"What do you mean?" Mr. D asked. "How did you get here?"

"The Owls rescued me," she said proudly. "They found out where I was and came and got me. They're heroes."

"I was the one who figured out how to get in," said Nish proudly, almost as if he expected any minute to be spelling his name for the newspaper reporters.

"But that's impossible," Mr. D sputtered. "We just met with the embassy people, and then Mr. Petrov and the Russian media showed up and he announced he had paid the ransom. He said you'd be released by the kidnappers tomorrow."

"Where were you?" Muck asked.

As best she could, Sarah explained. She told

them about the arena, about the tests, the scientists, the coaches, the girls. She told them how she'd been studied like she was some alien species. She said she hadn't been treated badly and that, in fact, one of the young Russian coaches had been the one to get them the key and set her free. He was a hero, she said.

The others filled in the blanks with shouts and boasts and laughter. Travis told about how they'd used Data's phone and the GPS. Dmitri told how he had reasoned with Pavel, and how Pavel said he had come to respect Sarah so much he couldn't stop them, how he decided, instead, to help.

Nish just wanted to talk about his own role in the adventure, how he had been the one who figured out how they could get into the rink when all the doors were locked.

"But who *were* they?" Mr. D asked. "Who would do such a thing?"

"There was one guy who seemed to be in charge," said Sarah. "I kept trying to see him, but I could never get close enough. He wore a hat really tight over his eyes. But I have this," she added. From her pack she pulled out Data's phone.

"I'll give it back to Data," Travis said.

"No," Sarah said. "Wait."

She fiddled with the phone and then held out the screen for all to see.

"I smuggled it into the last practice. I pretended I'd had the wind knocked out of me and went to the bench to loosen my equipment and catch my breath. I managed to sneak a picture of him watching. It's not very good, but that's him."

Everyone looked at the mysterious man in the photograph. His face wasn't very clear, but they could see he was tall. His fur hat was very distinctive.

"I know that hat," said Mr. D.

"So do I," said Muck.

Muck looked at the picture one more time, then started nodding.

"It's Mr. Petrov."

27

"We have a game to play," Muck announced after the police had been called and Mr. and Mrs. Cuthbertson had raced over from their hotel to see for themselves that Sarah was all right.

"We have a game to play . . . and we have our first-line center back."

There was no time for pausing. That evening, at the Ufa Arena, the Owls were up against Yekaterinburg, the top-rated Russian peewee team in the tournament.

There wasn't really a championship trophy – the gathering was supposed to be just a series of exhibition matches – but it was a tournament in the eyes and minds of the Owls. Winner would have "bragging rights," just like back in 1972, which seemed a million years ago to the young Owls.

The Owls scrambled to get their gear from their rooms and load it onto the shuttle bus that would take them to the rink. Sarah's equipment was ready for her, as carefully packed as she had left it. It smelled like roses compared to Nish's stinking equipment bag, which all the other Owls carefully avoided.

Nish was still boasting about his vital role in Sarah's rescue – "And then I remembered how the Zamboni had to dump its snow . . ." – as the bus turned in to the parking lot of the Ufa Arena. By then, every Owl on the bus was sick of listening to him. They'd tuned him out before the bus turned the first corner.

Travis felt happy. Happier than he could ever remember being. He was on his way to play a game of hockey against a strong team. He had his line back – Sarah in the middle, Dmitri on the right wing, Travis on left.

He thought about Pavel and why the young coach had decided to help them rather than turn them over to the bad guys. Pavel had been a bad guy himself, but then he turned out to be a good guy. Why? Was it just because he'd come to realize what an awful thing it was they were doing to her? Or had he been struggling with it all along?

It was going to be a good game. Travis had kissed the inside of his jersey as he hauled it over his head. He had been the first player on the ice, his skates the first to draw a line on the new, freshly flooded surface. He had twirled his stick perfectly as he pulled away. He had been first around the net, digging in extra hard as he exploded down the far side of the rink, his skates singing and sizzling. His first shot had pinged off the crossbar and high into the netting at the back of the Owls' net.

He was set.

"They're *good*!"

Sarah was gasping for breath. Her line had been trapped in its own end for the entire shift by the determined forechecking of the Yekaterinburg Dynamo. Travis had twice tried to clear the zone by firing the puck off the glass, only to have the tall defenseman for Dynamo leap into the air like a baseball outfielder and knock the puck down with his glove. But for the incredible goaltending of Jeremy – flopping this way and that, stacking his pads, moving quickly from post to post – Dynamo would have scored two or three times on that shift alone.

"Dmitri!" Travis yelled across Sarah's back. Dmitri leaned back and looked Travis's way.

"Use that speed of yours," Travis said. "We'll flip you the puck."

Dmitri nodded. The Screech Owl who had done all the talking when they rescued Sarah was again the silent Dmitri. Travis smiled, happy to be together with his line once again.

Travis saw Muck reach and gently tap Sarah's shoulder. The sign that her line was up next. Muck was going to double-shift them.

Andy's line came off after a puck went out of play, and Sarah jumped straight over the boards, not even bothering with the gate. She was ready.

Sarah easily won the face-off, blocking the other center with her butt while sliding the puck back to Lars. Lars hurried behind Jeremy's net, turned, and watched as everyone took up positions. The Dynamo forwards came over the blue line but swooped away like swallows, not challenging Lars.

Lars hit Nish on the far side with a pass, and the closest Dynamo player charged at him, hoping to cause a turnover. But Nish deftly sidestepped the check and tricked the player by doing absolutely nothing with the puck. He simply lifted his stick, leaving the puck where it was, and the checker roared by, stopping suddenly in a high spray of snow when he realized he'd just skated past a free puck.

Nish tapped a short pass to Sarah, who immediately wheeled and sent a hard backhand cross-ice to Travis. Travis had the open lane and moved fast over the Owls' blue line.

Dmitri was already away. Travis feared they'd be offside if he didn't get the Hail Mary pass away fast, so he flipped the puck immediately and it sailed high over his checker's head, over the reach of the tall defenseman, and landed smack on the blue line just as Dmitri crossed.

Dmitri was in alone. Travis felt he hardly needed to watch to know what would happen next: forehand fake, backhand, and high into the roof, the water bottle flying.

Muck never said a word. Just a light pinch of three players' shoulders when the line came off. For Travis, Sarah, and Dmitri, that was enough.

The highest praise possible from their coach.

They were tied 2–2 going into the third – Nish scoring on a power play blast from the point – and still tied with less than a minute to go in the game. A small touch to Sarah's shoulder from Muck sent her line over the boards again for the final shift of the game.

Travis was pumped. This wasn't a real tournament with a real championship to be won. It had been arranged by Ivan Petrov as an exhibition to show how good a peewee team could be with boys and girls playing together. It was to be an inspiration to girls playing the game in Russia, a country where girls were not allowed to play on teams with boys, and where many people still felt that girls were too delicate to play with stronger, larger boys. How silly, Travis thought. Find me a stronger Owl than Sam. Or a faster Owl than Sarah. Well, maybe Dmitri, but that would be all.

It had turned out that Ivan Petrov had more in mind than an exhibition. But that was all settled now and the games were still on.

The Owls wanted to win, badly.

Sarah took the face-off but lost it. The Dynamo center sent the puck back, and the tall Russian defenseman blew a hard slap shot that would have gone in the Owls' net had it not hit Jeremy's stick handle.

Was that luck? Travis wondered. Or was Jeremy that sharp tonight?

Didn't matter – the puck hadn't gone in. It slammed into the glass, where it lay in the corner.

Sarah was first there. She leaned down, placed the back of her stick blade on the puck, and scooped it up, causing a roar from the crowd.

She flipped the puck over the two checkers moving in on her, then quickly darted to pick up her own pass.

The crowd cheered.

Cheered? Travis wondered why. They were all Russians, apart from a handful of Screech Owl parents. He had no time to look up.

Sarah saw Travis cutting hard across center and threw a pass slightly behind him. Travis caught it in his skates and angled the puck up onto his stick. He slipped the puck between the skates of the closest checker and hit Dmitri with a perfect pass as Dmitri broke hard down the right side.

Dmitri was past the final defenseman so fast it looked as if he had gone through him like a ghost.

The defenseman, startled by Dmitri's speed, turned so abruptly in pursuit that he fell over.

Dmitri was in alone again. Travis could see it play out the way it always did: forehand fake, backhand, water bottle flying.

Only this time it didn't happen.

Dmitri drew out the goalie, who was anticipating this exact move, and the goaltender kept sliding while Dmitri kept skating, holding the puck instead of going to his backhand, and flying around the back of the net.

He could easily have scored on the wraparound, but Dmitri wasn't even looking at the net. He was searching for Sarah.

Sarah saw the play unfolding and charged to the net.

Dmitri threw a light saucer pass over the stick of the fallen defenseman. Sarah picked up the puck, stepped around the skates of the downed defender, slipped past the goaltender, still slightly out of his crease, and dropped the puck into the back of the net as if it were a little hamster she was patting back into its cage.

The crowd roared.

Travis was sure he could hear *"Sarah! Sarah! Sarah!"* being chanted as he and Dmitri, Nish, and Lars, and then Jeremy, piled onto Sarah in the corner.

He thought at first it must be the Owls still on the bench, but it sounded different, and it seemed to come from somewhere in the crowd.

He broke away and looked for the sound.

There, in the middle of the stands, was the entire Russian peewee girls' team, all decked out in their red tracksuits, all on their feet, yelling and screaming.

They were cheering for Sarah.

28

"What a devious plan."

Mr. Cuthbertson shook his head. Mrs. Cuthbertson was holding Sarah's hand and dabbing at her eyes, unable to hold back the tears.

All the Owls and the parents who had traveled to Russia had been called to a meeting in the Astoria to discuss the details of what had happened to Sarah.

Ivan Petrov's ambitions had taken control of his senses. He was fabulously wealthy thanks to his investments in oil – a billionaire several times over, as Mr. Yakushev said – but it was hockey that had made him famous in Russia. The money he had spent in support of Russian hockey had made him a much-loved public figure. And his stated intention to help develop women's hockey until it was on par with Canada and the United States had been very popular with the people. His picture was regularly in the papers, and he was often quoted. His fame in Russian hockey circles gave him a power that money could never buy.

But it wasn't enough just to help. He had to control the situation. He announced in the papers that, with his support and guidance, the Russian women's hockey team would dethrone the United States and Canada in the next Winter Olympics. He would pour as much money into the team as it took to get it to that level. He would use the best coaches, the best science – and this is where it began to spin out of control for him.

His plans were so complicated they fit together like a *matryoshka* doll – each one opening up to reveal another. The capturing of Sarah was just the first of many layers of his plan. He knew about Sarah's skill at hockey because he and another Russian had watched the Owls play in a tournament at Lake Placid. He had decided Sarah's ability to skate and pass made her the perfect model for Russian girls playing the game. He would have Sarah studied to a point where scientists could apply the best training and nutrition, and the coaches could give the best coaching to the top ten- to twelve-year-old girl players in the country. None of the girls themselves, or anyone connected with their team, needed to know that Sarah had been kidnapped.

That was his plan for women's hockey. Illegal – kidnapping a twelve-year-old girl – and a bit mad, but there was never any intention to harm Sarah in any way.

And this was where his plan for himself came in. He had her kidnapped. He then had the kidnappers (really himself) demand an outrageous ransom of ten million rubles – and he would come out of it a hero by paying off the ransom and getting Sarah back. It wouldn't cost him a cent.

But it all had blown up in his face after the Screech Owls stumbled upon his hockey rink laboratory and Pavel decided that he couldn't be part of it any longer and helped the Owls spring Sarah free. Petrov still might have succeeded in his plan had Sarah not been able to take that sneak photograph that allowed police and others to positively identify him.

It was such an incredible story that people all over Russia were shocked and horrified that one man's ambitions could take such a turn.

He was front-page news. Travis had grabbed a newspaper from the front desk of the Hotel Astoria, and he planned to keep it as a souvenir. It had a huge photograph of Ivan Petrov being hauled away by the police.

"What's the headline say?" he asked Dmitri, shoving the newspaper across a coffee table.

Dmitri looked down and smiled.

"It says, 'The New Ivan the Terrible.'"

CHECK OUT THE OTHER BOOKS
IN THE SCREECH OWLS SERIES!

PANIC IN PITTSBURGH

Travis's memory must be playing tricks on him! Did he really hear that someone is going to steal the Stanley Cup?

The Owls have been invited to Pittsburgh to compete in the biggest hockey tournament ever to be played on outdoor ice. The open-air tournament is to be held in the massive Heinz Field arena, home of football's mighty Pittsburgh Steelers. But almost as soon as the tournament begins, Travis suffers a serious concussion, just like the injury that sidelined Penguins' superstar Sidney Crosby. Travis is confined to his hotel room so his injured brain can recover. His memory is patchy, and he's having some weird dreams. So when he stumbles upon an outrageous plot to steal hockey's most coveted trophy, he can't be sure if his mind is playing tricks or whether the danger is a terrible reality.

FACE-OFF
AT THE ALAMO

The Screech Owls are deep in the heart of Texas, in the southern city of San Antonio. The town is a surprising hotbed of American ice hockey, and the Owls are excited to come and play in the big San Antonio Peewee Invitational. Between games, they can explore the fascinating canals that twist and turn through the city's historic downtown.

The tournament has been set up to include guided tours of the Alamo, the world's most famous fort, where Davy Crockett fought and died. The championship-winning team will even get to spend a night in the historic fort.

The Screech Owls discover that the Alamo is America's greatest symbol of courage and freedom, and when Travis and his friends uncover a secret plot to destroy it, they must summon all the courage of the fort's original defenders.

MYSTERY AT LAKE PLACID

Travis Lindsay, his best friend, Nish, and all their pals on the
Screech Owls hockey team are on their way to New York for an
international peewee tournament. As the team makes its way
to Lake Placid, excitement builds with the prospect of playing
on an Olympic rink, in a huge arena, scouts in the stands!

But as soon as they arrive, things start to go wrong.
Their star center, Sarah, plays badly. Travis gets knocked
down in the street. And someone starts tampering with the
equipment. Who is trying to sabotage the Screech Owls? And
can Travis and the others stop the destruction before the
final game?

THE NIGHT THEY STOLE THE STANLEY CUP

Someone is out to steal the Stanley Cup – and only the Screech Owls stand between the thieves and their prize!

Travis, Nish, and the rest of the Screech Owls have come to Toronto for the biggest hockey tournament of their lives – only to find themselves in the biggest *mess* of their lives. First, Nish sprains his ankle falling down the stairs at the CN Tower. Later, key members of the team get caught shoplifting. And during a tour of the Hockey Hall of Fame, Travis overhears two men plotting to snatch the priceless Stanley Cup and hold it for ransom!

Can the Screech Owls do anything to save the most revered trophy in the country? And can they rise to the challenge on the ice and play their best hockey ever?

THE GHOST OF THE STANLEY CUP

The Screech Owls have come to Ottawa to play in the Little Stanley Cup Peewee Tournament. This relaxed summer event honors Lord Stanley himself – the man who donated the Stanley Cup to hockey – and gives young players a chance to see the wonders of Canada's capital city, travel into the wilds of Algonquin Park, and even go river rafting.

Their manager, Mr. Dillinger, is also taking them to visit some of the region's famous ghosts: the ghost of a dead prime minister; the ghost of a man hanged for murder; the ghost of the famous painter Tom Thomson. At first the Owls think this is Mr. Dillinger's best idea ever, until Travis and his friends begin to suspect that one of these ghosts could be real.

Who is this phantom? Why has he come to haunt the Screech Owls? And what is his connection to the mysterious young stranger who offers to coach the team?

SUDDEN DEATH IN NEW YORK CITY

Nish has done some crazy things – but nothing to match this! At midnight on New Year's Eve, he plans to "moon" the entire world.

The Screech Owls are in New York City for the Big Apple International Peewee Tournament. Not only will they play hockey in Madison Square Garden, home of the New York Rangers, but on New Year's Eve they'll be going to Times Square for the live broadcast of the countdown to midnight. It will be shown on a giant TV screen and beamed around the world by a satellite. Data and Fahd soon discover that, with just a laptop and video camera, they can interrupt the broadcast – and Nish will be able to pull off the most outrageous stunt ever.

Just hours before midnight, the Screech Owls learn that terrorists plan to disrupt the New Year's celebration. What will Nish do now? And what will happen at the biggest party in history?

PERIL AT THE WORLD'S BIGGEST HOCKEY TOURNAMENT

The Screech Owls have convinced their coach, Muck, to let them play in the Bell Capital Cup in Ottawa, even though it means spending New Year's away from their families. It's a chance to skate on the same ice rink where Wayne Gretzky played his last game in Canada, and where NHLers like Daniel Alfredsson, Sidney Crosby, and Mario Lemieux have played.

During the tournament, political leaders from around the world are meeting in Ottawa. To pay tribute to the young hockey players, the prime minister has invited the leaders to watch the final game on New Year's Day. The Owls can barely contain their excitement!

Meanwhile, as Nish is nursing an injured knee off-ice, he may have finally found a way to get into the *Guinness World Records*. But what no one knows is that a diabolical terrorist also has plans to make it a memorable – and deadly – game.

Fred Lum / *The Globe and Mail*

ROY MACGREGOR was named a media inductee to the Hockey Hall of Fame in 2012, when he was given the Elmer Ferguson Memorial Award for excellence in hockey journalism. He has been involved in hockey all his life, from playing all-star hockey in Huntsville, Ontario, against the likes of Bobby Orr from nearby Parry Sound, to coaching, and he is still playing old-timers hockey in Ottawa, where he lives with his wife Ellen. They have four grown children. He was inspired to write *The Highest Number in the World*, illustrated by Geneviève Després, when his now grown-up daughter started playing hockey as a young girl. Roy is also the author of several classics in hockey literature. *Home Team: Fathers, Sons and Hockey* was shortlisted for the Governor General's Award for Literature. *Home Game: Hockey and Life in Canada* (written with Ken Dryden) was a bestseller, as were *Road Games: A Year in the Life of the NHL*, *The Seven A.M. Practice*, and his latest, *Wayne Gretzky's Ghost: And Other Tales from a Lifetime in Hockey*. He wrote *Mystery at Lake Placid*, the first book in the bestselling, internationally successful Screech Owls series in 1995. In 2005, Roy was named an Officer of the Order of Canada.